MIDWINTER MYSTERIES 2

Lincolnshire
COUNTY COUNCIL

COMMUNITIES, CULTURAL SERVICES
and ADULT EDUCATION
This book should be returned on or before
the last date shown below.

CMI

CM1 9/16		

To renew or order library books please telephone 01522 782010
or visit www.lincolnshire.gov.uk
You will require a Personal Identification Number.
Ask any member of staff for this.

EC. 199 (LIBS): RS/L5/19

MIDWINTER MYSTERIES 2

The second volume of *Midwinter Mysteries* continues the celebration of murder and mayhem.

There are bodies in the library and in the castle, buried secrets in the rose bed and on the battlefield. Cheats, con-men and charlatans stalk the pages of these baffling mysteries which are guaranteed to entertain and intrigue the reader. However, the best recommendation is the list of the contributors themselves: Gwendoline Butler, Desmond Cory, Clare Curzon, Antonia Fraser, Tim Heald, Reginald Hill, Graham Ison, Peter Lovesey, Shena Mackay, James Melville.

MIDWINTER MYSTERIES 2

Edited by
Hilary Hale

Magna Large Print Books
Long Preston, North Yorkshire, England.

British Library Cataloguing in Publication Data.

Edited by Hale, Hilary
  Midwinter mysteries 2.

A catalogue record for this book is
available from the British Library

ISBN 0-7505-0683-0

First published in Great Britain by Little, Brown & Co.,
Ltd., 1992

Copyright © 1992 by Little, Brown & Co., Ltd.

The stories are copyright respectively:
© Gwendoline Butler 1992   © Desmond Cory 1992
© Clare Curzon 1992   © Antonia Fraser 1992
© Tim Heald 1992   © Reginald Hill 1992
© Graham Ison 1992   © Peter Lovesey 1992
© Shena Mackay 1992   © James Melville 1992

Published in Large Print 1994 by arrangement with Little,
Brown & Co., Ltd.

Magna Large Print is an imprint of
Library Magna Books Ltd.
Printed and bound in Great Britain by
T.J. Press (Padstow) Ltd., Cornwall, PL28 8RW.

Contents

Editor's Note

The crime short story has remained a popular form of the whodunnit ever since the heyday of the form in the *Strand* magazine and the great American pulps. For the consumer it is always enlightening and, in a way, reassuring that people can be murdered on the page in so many different ways, for such a variety of motives and that the number of red herrings increases rather than diminishes with time.

Midwinter Mysteries 2 is ample witness to the ingenuity of contemporary crime writers to stretch the deductive powers of their readers, and to explore the complexity of the criminal mind. The collection is a celebration of the who—, how—, and whydunnit, and is a tribute to the mischievous imaginations of the contributors. I would like to thank them all for making this anthology such excellent entertainment and in this particular instance wish to record my special thanks for their patience and support during the early stages of bringing these stories together. The final result is proof that it was well worth while.

Hilary Hale

The Child Cannot Speak

Gwendoline Butler

Anna Miller, Derry Miller, these were the two that died. But the killing began before that. It began in someone's mind.

They were husband and wife. He was tall and very thin, she was short and inclined to be plump. Everyone knew them by sight in our village, although they did not speak much, concentrating on each other.

I used to see them out for their daily walks together, carrying the child in a kind of cradle suspended between them like a basket of fruit.

The child was heavy and knew she was their fruit because she smelt of them. She had known them first by their smell, her mother smelt of sweetness and milk, he smelt of smoke. Then she knew them by their voices and then by their names: Mama and Dada. She was Pet, Darling, Baby and occasionally, in an angry voice

Monster, Nuisance. But she had come to know more words than she could utter.

And she saw, she must have seen what took place, so the police said, and now held inside her that picture of the killing of her parents.

The killings in the comfortable cottage on the village street of Milderly in the beautiful county of Warwickshire. Rich farming country all around. Anna Miller was a farmer's daughter and knew all about guns, Derry took a gun out occasionally, but of the two, she was the better shot. We were all of farming stock, grew up with guns, understood them from a very early age.

A child who had seen her father murder her mother, then shoot himself cannot be the same as other children.

I was digging in my garden when I got the first intimation of what might happen.

Anna came and looked over the wall. We were friends, had been for years.

'What are you doing?'

As if she couldn't guess, a grave is a grave and always looks it even if small. 'Burying my cat.' I had never really liked Wotan, a vibrant and aggressive Siamese, but I liked burying him even less. Our two families employed a lean and handsome Scot as a part time gardener, I could have asked Gavin but for personal reasons preferred not to. He was an out of work actor from Glasgow with ambitions to be the next Sean Connery which he might achieve, he was very attractive. How expert he was as an actor, I do not know, but he had a high temper and strong sexual urge as I well knew.

'It was an accident,' Anna said quickly. 'Derry didn't mean it.'

Not sure about that. Derry had never liked Wotan.

'The car skidded. He would never kill.'

I put the earth over Wotan and patted it down. Then I planted some pansies on top. I didn't want him getting dug up. I didn't think Barney would do any such thing but he had intensely loved Wotan. Barney is my nephew, thirteen, but so small and slender, he looks younger. He'd catch up with the growing, I knew that, just give him time.

'We'll get Barney another cat.'

'Leave it alone. I would. You've got your hands full with Derry.'

Derry had such black depressions, such

13

swings of mood. I knew it worried her. 'He gets so angry,' she said.

'Not with you?'

'With everyone. He had a terrible row with Gavin.'

'Mutual, I should think.'

'Oh yes, Gavin gave as good as he got. Derry sacked him amidst threats on both sides.'

'He'll regret that.' I was thinking of their garden, wild and overplanted, not that Gavin was all that much help but some things he did do.

'He can't help it. It's like an itch in his mind. Never with Rose.'

'I should hope not.' Rose was their child, two and a bit.

'Mostly with his father.'

Ah his father, what would we do without a father to blame or hate? Or a mother. My parents had died young in a car crash when I was a teenager and Barney a very small boy and I did hold that against them, it was careless, prodigal. But they had left us enough to live on which made for forgiveness, for from what I knew of them, if they had not died then they might have spent it on cars and drugs and lovely trips. But with Derry it was his aggressive, successful policeman father. 'I thought his death would have cleared that up.'

'Worse, if anything.'

George Miller had died violently, stabbed to death by an ex-con with a grievance against him. He had always been an angry man but had usually held it in check, so I was told, professionally, directing aggression instead against his only son. Displacement activity, I believe it is called. Or is that when you give someone a long, hard kiss when you really want to bite them? I had a difficult lover myself, I hated being in love with a man so absent, so reclusive, but there it was.

'Louise, if anything happens to me, will you have Rose?'

I stopped planting pansies. 'Are you ill?'

'No, but you never know.' Anna sounded gloomy.

'Derry's infecting you with his moods. But about Rose...why me?'

'She's as much your child as mine.'

That was true. I'd looked after Rosie almost as much as her mother. She was a beautiful child.

From the bottom of the Miller's garden, Gavin was watching us with that professional brooding gaze of his which might

15

hide nothing at all. But he had his moods. In anger and resentment, he and Derry were well matched. There was a rumour in the village that he was Anna's lover. Or mine. Or had both of us. Gavin himself did nothing to disprove the rumour. He might have started it.

'Put it in writing,' I said, going back to my burying.

Thus Rose came to me with her inheritance, her clothes and her toys and behind her eyes, the knowledge of what she had seen.

There is always something odd to be observed in such cases of domestic murder. (I am a keen reader of murder trials and have a small library on them.) I think of the mutton in the house of the Bordens and the arsenic in that of the Maybricks. It was so in this instance.

The police who broke into the house to discover the bodies, to find Derry shot through the temple in one room and Anna shot in the side of her head in another, also discovered Rosie in her highchair.

Her eyes were bunged up as if she had been crying and crying and she was snuffling and sneezing.

Across the front of her yellow towelling bib was a bloody handprint. The killer had touched her, possibly considering her death too, then drawn back. The texture of the towelling prevented the handprint being read. Not a big hand, but then Derry had smallish hands.

One leather glove, the right one, had slipped from Derry's hands and lay on the floor by the gun. How strange he should have worn a glove, but he was always proud of his hands. It was a biggish glove, the sort you use in gardening, loose enough to have slid from his dead hand.

The WPC who brought Rosie over to me that night, thought that Rosie must have been crying for some time, her eyes were so swollen.

'She saw it all, poor kid, must have done.' She shook her head. 'But the child can't speak.'

Not quite true, Rosie knew a few words. 'Mama?' she said hopefully to me. She kept saying it, as if it was a relationship she had wanted to claim with me for a long time. I said No, and the WPC shook her head in sympathy, but the child still kept on saying Mama.

I was obliged to go to the Inquest to give evidence, since it was I who had called the police when the long silence in the Miller house began to worry me.

'You became anxious, Miss Drysdale?' said the coroner, a kindly old gentleman who practised a form of law in the county town. I say a form of law since he was better at advice and comfort than the strict letter of the law. He was excellent at helping you buy a house or make a will but on more complex matters he was better avoided: there has been so much legislation in the last two decades and he had not kept up as rigorously as he might have done.

He made a good local coroner though, because he knew everybody and usually knew all that had been going on behind the scenes.

'Yes, someone should have answered the bell.'

'And that was why you rang the police?'

'Yes.'

'But you have a key to the house?'

'Yes, Mrs Miller gave me one so that I could see to the post and so on when they were away.' Not that they went away often.

'And you did go into the house?'

I hesitated. 'Yes, I went into the hall. The sitting room door was open...and I saw a foot...I took a quick look.' This was when I had seen the glove on the floor. I stopped.

'Please go on, Miss Drysdale.' He nearly said Lu, he knew me so well. He lent me many books on trials and legal procedure, and forensic medicine, always an interest of mine.

'I didn't go any further...the house...it didn't smell very good, you know.' It had been a hot day.

I had gone back home and telephoned from there. So I did not see all that the police saw and what Rosie must have seen. I felt glad about that. I knew I could stand the sight of Anna and Derry dead, I had nursed once and knew about death, but after a long, hot day...yes, that I feared. Silly, of course. The fact of death is an absolute and it can't matter if hours have passed. But Anna and Derry dissolving into something else was what I could not face. They had been beautiful people, lovely to look at, Rosie got her looks from them.

Gavin was called and questioned but could add nothing to the story, he had been, he said, in Stratford all that morning auditioning for a part that he had got.

The police surgeon gave his evidence, the police gave theirs, the Millers' GP, Dr Archer, gave his, telling of Derry's dark depressive moods which, yes, alas, could have turned to violence.

The matter of the glove came up, was passed over, and not mentioned again.

Everyone in the village knew who Derry's father was and knew what they thought of him so there was a lot of sympathy for Derry. Less, oddly enough, for Anna who was thought to have been too hard on him.

Instructed by the coroner, the jury decided that Derry had killed his wife and then killed himself.

I went home, spoke to Rosie who was playing with Barney, who put small girls and cats in roughly the same category and petted them both. 'Look after Rosie,' I said. 'Don't let her get in a draught, I think she's got a cold.' And then I went out into the garden.

'Going gardening?' called Barney.

'Yes, it soothes the spirit.'

Not always though. I unlocked the garden shed, which I now kept locked although once I had not. There I drew open the drawer where I kept odds and ends of twine and insecticide and so on and where I stared down at a big leather glove, the left hand, and noted that there was no blood on it. Not used, this glove.

I was not going to destroy the glove, although I had no strong desire to keep it, but destroying it would have been an admission...of something. I admitted to nothing.

The garden shed was not always locked and everyone knew where I kept things. Almost everyone. Any person could have taken one glove and used it next door. Just as any person could have found Derry's gun which he always kept in an unlocked cupboard as if it was an umbrella.

So I went back into the house and took hold of Rosie, who must have seen a good deal of what went on in that house that day, but could not speak of it.

The case did not die down as might have been expected. Village gossip took it up and created a new version.

This story made out that Anna had killed her husband and then herself. Mrs Grieves in the Post Office let this out to me. It had been going round the village for some time but it had been kept from me. But in the end, Mrs Grieves said she 'thought I ought to know'. This is nearly always the preface to something you would rather never have heard.

'She killed him and then made it look as if he shot her.'

'How could she do that?'

'She was a farmer's daughter, she knew how to manage a shotgun. And it did lie between them on the floor. And he never had no gunpowder marks on his hand, I know that for a fact.'

'But he wore a glove.'

'All fake, my dear.'

'But wouldn't Anna's hands have been marked then?'

'She wore the glove, it was more her size, she had big hands.' She had, poor darling, and big feet.

The glove was determined to get into the act. It had a character of its own that right hand glove. I supposed it was still preserved in some police collection.

Waiting to be called for? What a horrid thought, as if it might get out and do another killing. Or join its fellow?

The gun too, that must be in some

police archive, and perhaps the two of them, glove and gun, might meet up and go out on some secret expedition. I pushed the thought back.

'But what motive could she have? Anna loved Derry,' I said savagely.

'Ah, that's it,' said Mrs Grieves, she gave me a sly look. 'He had another woman, you see. She was jealous.'

It was some days before I realised that the village had me named as the other woman. Someone painted *BITCH* in white paint on my garden wall. That hurt. I thought the village liked me.

That rumour was soon replaced with an even nastier one, in which I had killed both Anna and Derry, faking a suicide for him. The coroner was blamed for the way he directed the jury. 'Everyone knows George Fisher is past it and ought to retire.' This tale reached me secondhand through my new part time gardener (Gavin having gone to Shakespeare country) who did not name me as the murderess, but let me guess before filling in the background: 'His lady friend did it, and got away with it because she's good friends with the police.'

The bit about the police was news to me, although I had become friendly with

Sergeant Elliot who had investigated the double killing.

But parallel with this bit of the story was the news, retailed this time by Mrs Grieves once more, that 'the police are going to look into the case again... a man is coming down from London.'

I had it out with Mrs Grieves, you have to be strong with her. 'And why do they think I killed them both?'

'For the child,' she leaned over the counter, and lowered her voice: 'She's your child, ain't she, dear?'

The village had not got over the fact that Anna and I were both absent for a month and came back with Rosie. Never mind we did not travel together and did not arrive back together and that I had been in London and Anna in hospital in Oxford awaiting a difficult birth.

'Only in love,' I said firmly and loudly, so that the two ladies hanging over the magazines at the end of the shop and hoping to hear every word, jumped. For joy, I think. Something to pass on. 'Only Barney is a blood relation.'

There was a variation on this theme that popped up occasionally to the effect that Gavin had, as the village put it, 'got away with murder.' His motive was anger and jealousy.

Sergeant Elliot dismissed the idea of a 'man from Scotland Yard' arriving in the village, and said he would certainly have known and there was nothing in it.

All the same, I did wonder why he himself kept calling. I would look in my mirror and say, 'Well, you're not that pretty, girl, and you've lost a lot of weight, perhaps he just feels sorry for you.'

He was good to Barney, who was going away to school at his own request. Perhaps he was not too pleased at the arrival of Rosie in the house. I had several visits from a social worker, but Rosie had her own trust fund, her own solicitor to act as her legal guardian, and she was to be in my charge as Anna had requested. In writing.

Rosie was in good general health but she had a nasty little snuffle and we had several visits to the doctor, but eventually it died down.

As did the rumours and the gossip. With every month that passed, Rosie looked more and more like Anna and Derry and not in the least like me. She was their child, I just loved her, the village had to accept that as fact.

So gradually I ceased to be a bitch and the other woman, and became a heroine, one sacrificing her own life for the child.

I had not disposed of the glove, and there it sat in the drawer, by degrees becoming dryer and more wizened-looking. I could have thrown it away, but it might be found. I could have buried it, but that would have had its own dangers since the glove was of skin and skin seems to be preserved in the acid soil around here. I thought of putting it on the bonfire on Guy Fawkes Night, but it would smell. I just knew that glove would smell.

And all the time, in my house and in my care, was the child who had seen everything. I used to look at her and wonder what was buried in that memory of which she gave no sign but which one day might come bursting forth.

She started to walk and talk, and became ready for school, nursery class. She was a slow learner, but she got there in the end.

Later, she had a touch of asthma that cleared itself up without much medication, and a slight speech impediment, a kind of stutter which brought in the school psychologist, a small lady who lived in the village with her mother, Ada Duke, known to the children as the Duchess. She was interested in Rosie as a case history. Rosie who had seen so much and yet kept it hidden inside her.

'Do you think she'll ever say?'

The Duchess threw open her hands. 'Probably not. I don't think she can speak of it. But it's all there inside. Be better if it came out.'

Oh, do you think so? I thought. And for whom? I wasn't sure if I agreed with her. Bringing things out often meant only substituting other problems. Some things are better left buried, it seemed to me that the whole of civilisation depended on it.

'Watch her games, you can tell a lot from the games she plays.' The Duchess believed in play observation and play therapy.

Rosie had a doll's house, which had belonged to her mother, and several dolls and many soft toys, all of which she played with on her own and with her friends.

I became aware that with her friends, in public as it were, she played one sort of game, the usual childlike games, but on her own, she had a different style.

'That kid's weird,' Barney said one day. He had a robust attitude to toys himself:

27

break 'em and leave 'em was how he did it. And always win your game. I loved Barney very very much.

'Nonsense.' But I took it seriously enough to call on the Duchess.

'Better come and watch,' I said.

'Won't Rosie stop playing when she sees us?'

'No. Come and have a cup of tea at one end of the room and she won't notice. When Rosie plays she concentrates.'

When she played alone with her doll's house, Rosie turned all the furniture to the wall, drew any curtains that there might be, and then assembled all the small objects like the cooking pots on the miniature stove, the china set out for dinner on the table, the little dressing-set by the bed, all these things she laid in rows on the floor of the downstairs room. Then one by one, she washed them. Then she put them back, she rearranged the house. It was painstakingly and lovingly done. If she did not have time to finish the job, then she covered everything with paper tissues until she could get back to it.

Nothing was said, speech was not part of the game.

When she played with her dolls or

soft toys, she made them paper hats and covered their eyes. 'They like it like that,' she said, if asked. Questions were not invited. 'Naughty,' she said to her masked toys.

The Duchess said that the play showed Rosie felt guilty.

I protested. 'She's only a baby.'

'Guilt can be acquired young,' said Miss Duke.

Or even inherited, I thought, remembering Derry. He had been loaded down with guilt, but it was not his own guilt, he had nothing to be guilty of, it was his father's guilt he was bearing. Now it seems it was Rosie's turn, her inheritance, absolutely useless, indeed an impediment, something to drag behind you like a third leg.

'No one has told her what happened to her parents.'

'But she has taken in more than we know. Perhaps everything. She feels it. Maybe it is no more than a shadow at the back of her mind, a shapeless form, but it is there.'

And one day a shape might take a name, I thought, but I did not say so.

The house next door was sold after a long gap, no local wanted to live in it, and the money went into Rosie's estate, but the family that moved in did not stay many months. Not a happy house, they said. Of course, the village had been talking to them.

Another family tried the house, but the husband died, so they too did not stay. A solitary woman bought the house next, she stayed a short while but said the garden was too much for her. It was a wilderness.

The house was empty for some time after Miss Baxter left. She had planted a few roses but even these seemed sad.

Rosie was growing up and so was Barney. No longer a baby but not quite a little girl yet... I could see Rosie admired Barney for being so big and manly (he had made up for his slow start) and he thought Rosie was a beauty in the making. Her speech improved, her stutter nothing more than a slight, attractive drawl. The games with her dolls and their house were suspended. I say suspended because the little house and her main collection of soft toys and dolls were hidden beneath a sheet she had draped over them, they were still muffled. Did she think life was going on inside there? Sometimes she looked at the drapery as if she thought so. I began to worry how she would handle sex, and how Barney would for that matter. Not easy for either of them, I thought.

At her request, I never touched her toys. She no longer called me Mama, but Aunt Lu. I still had the glove, unchanged by its sojourn in the drawer in the garden shed.

'You never wear gardening gloves now, Lu,' Barney said one day when I was weeding. 'And your hands show it.'

'No,' I looked down at my poor battered hands, scarred with this and that from family life, mute confessions to a lot I had gone through. 'Funny, isn't it, Barney, I don't seem to fancy them.'

Barney smiled and shook his head. 'You're the funny one, Lu.'

Rosie and Barney treated each other with interested reserve, but young as they were underneath was a current that ran strong and might grow into something stronger.

I took action that day. Plucked the glove from the drawer where it hid and climbed the garden fence to what had been the Miller's garden.

I would bury the glove in the most suitable spot. I dug a hole under one of the blighted roses and popped it in. It still looked like a glove, flat and empty. I hoped it stayed that way.

Oh Rosie, Rosie, I thought, what a lot I have done and dared that perhaps you would have been better without. They were a disaster, your parents, but they were yours and perhaps you should have been left with them. But I mustn't pass judgement, these things happen.

Sergeant Elliot had always kept in touch. He was interested, he said, he wanted to see how Rosie got on, what she might say one day. He was hard to keep out, I liked him, more than liked him, you see. A nice, tough, well-mannered man who deserved the promotion which made him an Inspector, and someone in line for even higher promotion. But he could be remote and inaccessible at times.

One day he called to say that he had bought the house next door, and did I mind? Glad to have you for a neighbour, I said, which was both true and untrue.

He brought with him his dog, a terrier with a hint of spaniel and a touch of a truffle hound. We saw more of each other then, went to the theatre, to occasional concerts, I liked Mozart, he liked Richard

Strauss, so we usually chose Beethoven and Schubert, you could settle for that.

'I never see Barney these days.'

'He's gone to live with his grandmother, he's getting extra coaching for his university, he wants to be a vet and that is a tough school to get into.'

'You have to like animals too.'

'Loves 'em,' I said. 'But he's not sentimental. Doesn't make gods out of dogs.'

Tim Elliot gave me a reproachful look. 'But I'm not like that with Buster.'

Tim Elliot and Louise Drysdale became known as a couple in the village which did not know what to make of it, especially Mrs Grieves who had a wry look on her mouth as if she was eating an acid drop when she sold me stamps across the counter.

My policeman was not a keen gardener which was a virtue in my eyes, but he did a little weeding. I used to keep a watch on him but he never dug deep. He came back one day with a rose tree and asked my advice.

'Where should I put it? There's a kind of rosebed.'

'I shouldn't put it there, overcrowded

33

already.' As indeed it was with Miss Baxter's sad relics, never mind what else that might be souring the ground.

'I fancy up here by your fence,' he said with a grin. He patted the fence, which was broken, it was where Anna and I had always passed through. Gavin too for that matter. 'It's called The Doctor, this rose, and it sounds healthy.'

Buster had taken himself off to the rosebed and was rooting away in the soil.

'I should stop that dog doing that,' I said.

'Oh, he's only looking for bones.' He gave Buster an indulgent look. 'I think he's found something. Clever boy.'

Clever boy, I thought grimly, as Buster deposited his find at his master's feet.

Brown, earth stained, unpleasing, it was unmistakably a bit of old mutton, but it made me realise what I must do.

Next day, early in the afternoon because Barney was coming to tea, I left Rosie to her own employment, reading and painting by the window (she was home from school with a touch of that chest trouble), and went to dig in the earth where Buster had been before me. I knew which rose to go for, it had the most mildew. I guessed I

34

would find what I was looking for without much trouble, easy to find, that glove.

A barking figure hurled itself across the garden, followed by Tim Elliot himself.

'What are you doing, Lu?'

I sat back on my heels, glove in my hand. I should have burnt it or cut it up, long since.

'I thought you were out.' I took up the glove, it was moist and heavy, memories heaped themselves upon it and made it hard to handle. It seemed to slip between my fingers.

Tim Elliot took it up. His eyes, dark brown and very bright, looked from it to me. He did not pretend not to understand. 'In the house?'

I stood up. 'Yes, let's go.' I felt as though I was under arrest.

My sitting room was full of the afternoon sun, a pile of Rosie's books on the window seat, but she was not there herself. I put the glove down by the fire, where it immediately began to smell but shrank in importance. What was a glove after all?

I sat down on the sofa by the fire and Tim Elliot sat opposite me. 'Where's the child?'

'Upstairs, in the garden, I don't know.'

'It's the death of her parents we shall be talking about.' He didn't sound as friendly and gentle as usual. And not remote at all but highly concentrated on me and the present moment.

'We don't speak of it to her.' But the shade of it was there for her, always had been. 'She knows there was a terrible accident.'

'She was there.'

'I know that, damn it.'

'But there's one thing I ought to say, one mercy about it: from the position of the highchair she must have heard but may not have seen.'

Thank God, I thought.

'I think you ought to know that the police were never satisfied with the idea that Derry Miller killed his wife and then himself... There should have been traces on his hands if he had used the gun. There were none.'

'The glove...' I said.

'Oh yes, on the glove. Whoever used the gun, used the glove.' He got up and kicked the glove. 'The pair to this. Your glove, I must assume from your behaviour.'

I bowed my head. 'I didn't kill them.'

We would never come to anything now

as a couple, I thought, and grieved for it, he was such a lovely man. Nicer by far than others I had loved, Derry, Gavin.

'There were certain things that didn't come out at the inquest... The post mortem showed that Anna Miller had the beginnings of a degenerate disease... She may have felt some forewarning of this.'

'I think she did.' I was remembering what she had said to me when she asked me to take Rosie. Poor Anna.

'So it seemed possible that she had killed her husband and then killed herself. We worked on that, but the position of the wound in her head made it improbable. Not impossible but improbable.'

He stared down at the glove. Outside, I could hear Buster sniffing at the door. Let him stay, he had done enough damage. But for him I would never have dug up the glove.

'And so if both of them were killed, and it was not suicide and murder, then it was double murder by someone unknown. Someone who came into the house, who knew how to use a gun and had the twin to that glove there.'

'My glove, but I didn't do it.'

'I never thought that, Lu. Some of the

others did, but not me... But you knew who could have done. Did you love Gavin Easton so very much?'

I shook my head. 'No,' I breathed. I knew how to love, I had loved Derry, bitterly, angrily, tenderly. But not to kill for. I loved Rosie, I loved Barney, but what I had felt for Gavin was more a kind of lust. Of which I was now ashamed. But there was a deeper, better love than that.

Behind the curtain the child, Rosie, heard all this and was listening. The shadows that had dwelt inside her for so long had been given a name. Dead mother, dead father, smelling of themselves and of blood and the other smell pungent and nose pricking which had followed after a noise, a bang, which had grown fainter in her ears as the years passed. The smells had remained, the smell which was herself, and that other smell of that other person. Who smelt familiar, part of everyday life, whom one had always known. The person who smelt that way had been there, was part of the memory.

Her body had known and remembered.

Rosie heard the man say to Aunt Lu, 'What a pity the child could not speak.'

Behind the curtain Rosie thought but the child can speak. I know who was there that day. I have always known. I knew the smell, I knew the feeling. Her nose had known, her chest had known, she had sneezed and wept with her knowledge. I have always known and Auntie Lu must have known.

She looked down the garden path to where Barney was coming with his new Siamese cat on his shoulder, and something sharp stirred in her mind as she began to sneeze and snuffle and wheeze.

Barney, who had had cat hairs on his jacket when he had avenged the death of Wotan, walked forward confidently.

I didn't mean to kill her, he told himself as he advanced towards Rosie whom he could see behind the curtain staring out at him, I would never have killed the baby nor her mother, but her mother came screaming at me when she saw the gun. Only a cat, she said, only a cat. Derry Miller was different, I knew he'd killed Wotan on purpose. I used his gun and Lu's glove, I knew about powder marks from one of Lu's books, real murder library Lu has.

I'll make it all right, I would never really harm a woman or child, but Wotan was something special. I wouldn't do it now, of course, he told himself, only a kid then. But he did not regret it. It had been right in its time.

He gave a smile and a wave as he hurried towards Rosie who was already planning her revenge.

'Aunt Lu,' she called, coming out from behind the curtain. 'Something to tell.'

Switchblade

A Professor Dobie story

Desmond Cory

'Abjure rhetorical flourishes, Dancey. *Abjure* them, I say.' Professor Crane's high-pitched lecture-hall voice had taken on an aggrieved tone that Dancey found all too familiar; he sighed inwardly. 'Abstain from all such indulgences. Brevity, remember, is of the essence.'

'Yessir,' Dancey said, wondering (such is the intolerance of youth) when the silly old fossil was going to get to the point.

'For instance, you say—and I quote— "Indeed when the Emperor Julian met his death, it was upon a Roman sword wielded by a Christian fanatic." Your concern for rhetorical effect, you see, has led you here into inaccuracy. Since the primary sources, as you point out earlier, indicate that Julian was fatally wounded in the course of a cavalry skirmish, it is almost impossible

41

that he should have been killed by a Roman *sword*. A Roman *spear*, boy, a Roman *spear*.'

'I see, sir. But that doesn't really affect the point—'

'In fact you consistently *fail* to see, Dancey, and that is because you lack the capacity to argue from clear historical evidence and to find empirical justification for your arguments.' Crane rose creakily to his feet. 'Such as *this*.'

Dancey watched him lift the lid of the glass display cabinet (undoubtedly pinched from the Classical library just outside his study door, but now placed conveniently behind the professorial desk) and groaned to himself; he was vaguely familiar with the contents of Crane's Pandora's box—a random collection of hideous objects all in their different ways expressive of their owner's obsession with Roman military history, a preoccupation which Dancey himself in no way shared. There were swords, daggers, spearheads, arrow-points... All kinds of miscellaneous junk. Crane, he saw, was reaching inside to withdraw a sinister-looking artefact; this he then plonked down on his desk and on top of Dancey's offending essay.

'*This* is the weapon, Dancey, that the legions carried the length of the Roman empire, from Scotland to Persia. The arm upon which Julian based his attempt to carry the frontiers of that empire through Persia into India and thus to outdo the achievements even of Alexander. Right, Dancey?'

'Yes, sir. But—'

'*Wrong,* Dancey. Julian was a cavalry commander. All the authorities comment on the remarkable speed with which he moved and manoeuvred his armies—that was the secret of his military genius. Observe this weapon. No—pick it *up,* boy. *Examine* it.'

Dancey did so, cautiously. He didn't ask if it were authentic; it obviously was, and in good condition. It was heavier than he'd expected, and considerably shorter. 'Is this of the, er...period, sir?'

'A good question, and germane to the issue, although the standard design altered, as you should know, very little over five centuries. In fact that particular sword appertains quite certainly to the third century AD. You'll notice at once that it's a stabbing, not a slicing weapon—unlike the broadsword used by the Germanic tribes—and that the blade is very much shorter than that of a modern rapier. It's therefore an effective weapon at close quarters—an *infantry* weapon, in fact. But remarkably ineffective against cavalry, as Julian must have realised. We might say that his revolutionary concept of warfare depended on his realisation that the Roman sword simply couldn't *reach* a man on a moving horse. The point is easily proved.' Crane clambered energetically, if not agilely, on top of his desk and began to sway his body to and fro, like a limbo dancer suddenly assailed by delirium tremens. Dancey stared at him, open-mouthed. 'Come on then, Dancey. *I* am the Emperor Julian. *You* are the Christian assassin you allege. Let's see if you can pink me a sweet one.'

Dancey rose to his feet with alacrity, his fist clamped sweatily round the sword hilt. 'You mean you want me to...?'

'No hacking, mind. No vulgar swiping. No stabbing at the legs, either. And don't forget that if this were for real I'd be wearing a breastplate. The neck or under the armpits—*those* are the vulnerable points. *Go* for them, boy.'

'Okay,' Dancey said, trying out an experimental swish. 'Have at thee, professor.'

'... Never seen anything like it in all my puff,' Copleston said. 'There was the old boy dancing about on top of his desk with young Dancey prodding away at him with some kind of a...*sword* or something...As I said at the time, I thought they'd both gone bonkers. Turned out it was only the Professor trying to make history come alive, as he puts it. Of course he got down off the desk as soon as he saw me and even had the grace to look a bit abashed about it. But—'

'Disconcerting.'

'Yes. Mind you, I've got used to that sort of thing since I've been in charge of the classical texts here, but I don't know that the students really *like* it. Dancey didn't, anyway. He looked pretty furious when he came out ten minutes later. "One of these days I *will* kill the old bugger"—that's what he said. Naturally I never supposed—'

'Well, *somebody* did,' said Detective Inspector Jackson.

Emerging from Copleston's minuscule

office, where he had been phoning a brief and not very coherent situation report through to Central, Jackson paused to cast a glance round the Classical library. It wasn't a large room and, being well cluttered up with bookshelves, high bookcases and reading tables, seemed even smaller than it was; at the far end an open door—invisible from the Librarian's rabbit-hutch—gave onto the late Professor Crane's study, where various scuffling sounds and muttered imprecations suggested the Scene-of-Crime boys to be still at work, though the body itself had been efficiently carted off some fifteen minutes ago. No question, of course, as to the cause of death and very little, at least in Jackson's mind, as to the perpetrator, who now sat at one of the nearby reading tables looking, as might be expected, cheesed off. Young Dancey had a nasty temper, from all accounts. Recent events might be held to have proved that contention.

The library was at the moment otherwise very sparsely inhabited. Seated over in the far corner behind a towering pile of antiquated volumes was a bespectacled and somewhat frail-looking young lady who, despite the stir of activity in the study beside her, was continuing unconcernedly to make notes in a loose-leaf notebook; a well-conducted person, evidently, and one with remarkable powers of concentration. Jackson knew about *her*. He had her name written down in *his* notebook and she could, despite appearances, turn out to be his star witness. She'd better be. There didn't seem to be any others, except for what's-his-name, the librarian chap. Copleston. It didn't matter. This time, Jackson had his charlie on toast. That was all he knew and all he needed to know, at least for the moment. Unless, of course...

The only other occupant of the room was an unruly-haired man of mildly benevolent aspect who was standing by one of the bookcases leafing through the pages of some ancient and manifestly mouldering volume. Him Jackson now approached. 'What in heaven's name are *you* doing here, Mr Dobie?'

Nemo petit modicus que mittebantur amicis a Seneca,' Dobie said reprovingly (if bewilderingly), *'qua Piso bonus, quae Dobieus solebat largiri.* I can't put it fairer than that.'

'I thought you was Mathematics.'

'I am,' Dobie said, cautiously restoring

47

Juvenal to his appointed place on the bookshelf. 'But Croaker and I are of old acquaintance. We went to the same college—'

'Croaker?'

'Professor Crane, I should have said.'

'Ah.' Jackson was relieved, having for a moment supposed the other to be referring to some bloody Latin poet or other, well, you never *knew* with Professor Dobie. 'Then maybe you can fill me in on a few details. Me being a little bit out of my depth here, so to speak.' Dobie might, he thought, also be of use to him in dealing with the Rector, whose arrival upon the scene was momently threatened and who might well react unfavourably to the news that one of his students was about to be arrested. 'Mind you, we've got our charlie. *That*'s not the problem. But—'

'Your charlie? *What* charlie?'

'Him over there.'

'Dancey?' Dobie shook his tousled head, more in sorrow than in anger. 'No, no, no. *He* didn't do it.'

'I *knew* you'd say that,' Jackson said.

'Now then.' Ensconced once more in Crane's study and out of Dancey's earshot,

Jackson was reverting to type in his agitation. 'This isn't one of your classical locked-door John Carson Dick stories, Mr Dobie. Nothing like that. Get all those ideas out of your pretty little...out of your head. Here's what happened, near as I can make out. Twelve o'clock on the dot, along comes that young fellow outside with what they tell me is a Roman sword, if you'll credit it, tucked under one arm and some folders and suchlike under the other. Knocks on the door, goes in. Couple of minutes later, out he comes, goes over to that chap Copleston's office in that library place outside, tells him this Crane geezer's been killed. So he has. With that Roman sword thing stuck right through him; near as nothing.'

Jackson nodded towards the chalked outline beside the desk and the very evident bloodstains on the worn brown carpet. The Scene-of-Crimes lot had by now folded their tents (like the Arab) and silently stolen away, but not without—as always—leaving substantial indications of their recent encampment on the site. Sergeant Evans seemed to have left fingerprint powder almost everywhere, the clumsy clot.

Jackson wiped his fingers stoically on a handkerchief and continued.

'Dead within seconds, according to Paddy Oates. Stabbed from behind while seated at his desk. Looks like he was marking papers or something, but that's beside the point. Sword's got a nice clear set of Dancey's prints on the hilt and no-one else's, which is what you'd expect since there was no-one else in the room at the time. All that's left to do is read him his rights, far as I'm concerned. But what I— What are you shaking your head about *now?*'

'I don't understand,' Dobie said, 'why he was carrying that thing around in the first place. Students aren't allowed to bring offensive weapons to tutorials, for obvious reasons.'

'Ah. *That's* what he was so steamed up about. Seems he was here earlier this morning for a...what you said, a lesson.'

'A tutorial.'

'Right, and he made some kind of bloomer which had to do with someone being killed by a Roman sword...so the professor gave him an extra *assignment*, is that right?' Jackson was consulting his notebook rather anxiously. 'Told him to

50

write a full report on the characteristics of the Roman sword, find out its length and weight and all that stuff and gave him an hour to do it in. So that's what—'

'And did he?'

'I suppose so. It'll all be in those folders he was carrying.' Jackson nodded towards the desk. 'Left them behind, he did, being in a bit of a panic, I shouldn't wonder. Left the sword behind, too, of course. In the professor.' It was, Dobie saw, also on the desk; rather obviously, the blade hadn't been cleaned. 'Shouldn't touch it, Mr Dobie, if I were you.'

'I wasn't going to. It's a nasty-looking weapon.'

'Makes a nasty-looking wound, I can tell you. Well, look at all that blood. And it's a good job it's such an open-and-shut business because the Super's going to want a quick arrest before all the stories start flying around. I mean, you know even better than I do what these students are like.'

And indeed the wildest of rumours were already circulating through the Junior Common Room.

'Old Copleston heard him shout out, *Et*

tu, Brute?... And when he went in there was Croaker lying on the floor, all boltered in blood like Banquo, great big pool of it spreading out over the carpet...'

'Oh eccchhh! That's *gross!*...'

'And there was Dancey whirling this Excalibur thing round his head and quoting Aeschylus at the top of his voice...'

'Oooooo Terence, you *are* awful. I don't believe a word of it.'

Nobody knew *what* to believe. That was the trouble.

Dobie had not, in fact, been a particularly close friend of Professor Crane (whose nickname made no reference, as might have been supposed, to any vocal peculiarity or idiosyncrasy of the Professor's but was commonly held to have originated in an ill-timed reference, made earlier in his academic career, to some misbegotten comic drama by benighted Aristophanes, whom he had at that moment inexplicably confused with Aristotle). A similarly confused situation, however, had once again clearly arisen and it was no less clearly Dobie's duty, as a senior member of the University, to do what he could to confuse it still further, if possible.

Accordingly, he asked, 'What *about* the other students.'

'What other students?'

'You've got a young lady sitting out there—'

'Oh yes. Miss Hearne, her name is. She's been sitting there most of the morning, writing an essay on someone called Julian the Apostrophe.'

'Julian the Apostate. Really, Jacko, if you'd ever—'

Jackson was unrepentant. 'A prostate, a postulate, a little yellow phosphate, what's it matter? It all comes of having to get my notes down too quick. Point is, it makes her a witness.'

'To what?'

'To the fact that Professor Crane was alive and kicking at a quarter to twelve, which is when she went into his study to borrow a book. No-one else went in there until Dancey arrived, and what's more no-one else went into the room between eleven—which is when Dancey left—and twelve o'clock, when he came back. She says so, and Copleston bears her out. In fact he can't see the study door from where he sits, the bookcases get in the way—I've checked on that myself—but he can see the *library* door all right, he's right beside it. And as there's no other entrance to the place, it amounts to the same thing.'

'Curious. I suppose no-one could have got in through—'

'Forget it.'

Dobie looked at the formidably barred study windows and shook his head. 'Valuable texts in the Classics library, of course. And quite a few in Croaker's own collection, if it comes to that. So some effort has had to be made to discourage theft. Which book did she borrow?'

'*I* dunno. What's it matter? She said she wanted to copy a reference, whatever that means.'

'It means she...Ah.' Dobie's lacklustre gaze, which had drifted from the window to the bookshelf behind the desk, detected a gap in the closely-packed volumes and brightened slightly. He moved across to pick out a small leather-bound text and riffled through the pages. 'I see. Shaftesbury's *Treatises*, quite so. Original three-volume edition of 1758, yum. Interesting. Volume Two is missing, as you see. Well, that explains it.'

'Explains what?'

'Why she wanted to borrow the book.

54

It's in English, of course. Only Greek and Latin text out there in the library, so she couldn't have... But it's still a little puzzling—'

'Mr Dobie, you're *dithering* again.'

'Perhaps I am.' Dobie seated himself wearily on the swivel chair behind Crane's desk, staring down at the sheaves of marked and unmarked essays strewn over its surface. Jackson, about to protest, thought better of it and sat down on the harder wooden chair placed, for the convenience of visiting students, directly opposite. He tried to visualise Professor Crane perched on top of the paper-littered desk, ducking this way and that as Dancey... An eccentric old bird, as was obvious. But then they *all* were, in this place. Especially Dobie: who, when you thought about it, was in a class by himself.

'I am,' Dobie announced, 'Convenor to the University Disciplinary Committee, I'm sorry to say.'

Oh lummy, Jackson thought. He's off again. 'I'm sorry if *you*'re sorry, Mr Dobie, but I don't see—'

'I was calling on Professor Crane this morning in an official capacity. To discuss what course of action to be taken with regard to one of his students who he believed to be cheating the examiners.'

Wait a minute, Jackson said to himself, now *wait* a minute, he could be on to something after all... *'Which* student?'

'He didn't say. He only said that he was convinced the student in question was plagiarising.'

'Good God!' Jackson stared in revulsion towards the door behind which Dancey, presumably, still forlornly sat. 'The filthy little swine. But shouldn't the Public Health authorities—'

'Copying,' Dobie kindly explained, 'somebody else's work. And passing it off as your own. It's a very serious offence in University circles, though sometimes one has to draw a very fine line... However, I mention the matter only because it may have some relevance to the present situation. If you think—'

'I should say it has. The one thing we didn't have was a really adequate *motive* for... If you could show that he was... A serious offence, you said? Would he be expunged for it?'

'Expelled, yes, certainly. Or sent down, as we put it. And it would have very grave repercussions on that student's future career. But don't get *too* excited, Jacko. Sometimes students get sent down without murdering their tutors in reprisal. It's been known to happen.'

'But it *is* a motive?'

'A motive, yes. But not necessarily Dancey's.'

Jackson clicked his tongue. 'Mr Dobie... It just couldn't have been anyone else.'

'Oh yes, it could,' Dobie said. 'Perhaps I could have a chat with your charlie, if you don't mind.'

Dancey was recalcitrant to begin with and even morose, but that wasn't surprising in the circumstances. Since, however, it was obvious to him (as it would have been to anyone) that Dobie wasn't a policeman, he soon stopped muttering sullenly about wanting to see his solicitor and before very long became positively garrulous. As he talked, his right knee kept jumping up and down; he seemed to be in a high old state of nerves but that, again, was hardly surprising. '... Of course I didn't kill him. He wasn't killed with that old sword at all. He was dead when I got there...lying there behind the... It's all some kind of a fix-up. That cop, he's trying to fix it so I... He

57

must be. It doesn't make sense.'

'Then let's try to get it a little clearer,' Dobie said. 'You see, the Inspector tells me you were seen to go into the study, but he says it was a couple of minutes before you came out again. Now if, as you say, when you went in you saw he was dead already—'

'I don't think it was as long as that but the point *is*, I didn't see him at once. Not right away. Because he was down behind the desk, you see. I thought maybe he'd gone out for some reason. So then I thought, well, I'll leave my assignment paper and the bloody...sorry, that sword of his on the desk for him and I sort of moved forwards and *that* was when I...'

'And did you?'

'Did I what?'

'*Did* you leave those things on his desk?'

'I must have done. Put them down there, anyway. I don't really remember clearly *what* I did. I think I just *stood* there for a bit...I wasn't even looking at *him* or I don't think so, it was all rather...horrible. As far as I can recall, I was sort of staring out of the window, it was—'

'A bit of a shock.'

'Yes, it was. Then I thought, better tell

someone about it, call for an ambulance or something, so that's what I did. I told Mr Copleston.'

'Where was he?'

'Where he always is. That little...hardly an office, is it? More of an alcove sort of place. Anyway he's got a telephone there so he rang the ambulance service and then the police and he—'

'He believed you, did he? He didn't go and check in the study for himself?'

'No. He said it'd be better not to go in or touch anything because... Well, all that *blood*. That's why he rang the police as well as the... Well, naturally.'

'What about Miss Hearne? Did she say or do anything?'

'Freda? Well, that's right, she was working over in the far corner...I don't think she realised what was going on, not till later when the police got here. Too wrapped up in what she was doing, perhaps.'

'What *was* she doing?'

'I don't know. I didn't really notice. Working on an essay, maybe... She had a lot of books piled up on her table, but then she always has.'

'A serious student, is she?'

59

'Oh yes. One of old Croak...Crane's favourites, anyway. Has her down for a First, I would imagine.' Dancey considered the matter. 'Yes, Freda's a worker all right. She's got great powers of concentration. I wish *I* had 'em.'

'Perhaps if you really applied yourself. For instance, when Professor Crane got up on this desk and asked you to—'

'Oh, you heard about *that?*' For the first time Dancey smiled, if only faintly. 'Yes, that was weird. Still, he did manage to prove his point.'

'Which was?'

'Oh, that it isn't very easy to stab a man on horseback with one of those Roman swords. In fact, it's nearly impossible. They're too *short,* is why, and much heavier than you'd think... You could hack at a horseman's legs all right, or at a pinch you could try to stab the horse, I suppose...'

'It's amazing, though, what you can do in the heat of battle. When—as I say—you're concentrating on the job in hand. You weren't *really* trying to kill the Professor, were you?'

'Of course not. Just to see if the sword point would *reach* him. And it wouldn't.

60

Not so as you could stab him *properly* with it. Not without jumping right up into the air.'

'Just so,' Dobie said. 'Quite.'

'Shaftesbury,' said Freda Hearne, blinking at Dobie from behind her bifocal lenses, 'refers to Julian as "that virtuous and gallant Emperor...treacherously assassin-ated by one of his Christian soldiers..." and indeed the historical record would speak for itself if the blind dogmatism of the Christian church had ever allowed it to do so. What I'm wondering right now is if the blind dogmatism of the local constabulary is ever going to allow *me* to go and get some lunch. I'm *starving* and I don't see how I can add very much to what I've told the Inspector already.'

'Sometimes,' Dobie said, 'dogmatism is confused with self-interest, don't you think? Actually I'm not familiar with the passage you just quoted. This, I take it, is the book you...? Yes. Most interesting.' He opened it and stared uncertainly at the title page. 'Shaftesbury, of course—'

'He quotes Julian's letter to the Bostrenes in full. But you needn't bother to look it up. I've been copying out what I take to be the relevant passages. This one, for instance. "It is by DISCOURSE and REASON, not by *blows*, *insults*, or *violence*, that men are to be informed of truth, and convinced of error." Those sentiments should appeal to you, Professor Dobie, as a mathematician.'

'Indeed they do. But clearly they had no such appeal to the assassin you mentioned—or, for that matter, to whoever brought Professor Crane's distinguished career to a similar unfortunate conclusion. What exactly was he *doing* when you last saw him?'

'He was marking what I took to be students' essays and giggling to himself as he did so.'

'Yes, I'm afraid tutors do on occasion display these regrettable sadistic tendencies. He was seated at his desk, of course?'

'Where else? I asked if I could borrow Shaftesbury's *Treatises* for an hour or so and he just nodded towards the bookshelf and I walked over and helped myself...and that was that.'

'Did he lend you books in that way very often?'

'Fairly often, yes. Maybe two or three times a month.'

Dobie flipped the book shut and put it down on the reading table. 'And I understand you were so engrossed in this particular volume that you remained unaware of young Dancey's, er...*discovery* until some little while later?'

Miss Hearne flushed a becoming shade of pink. 'Yes, that's true. I know it sounds odd but I *do* get wrapped up in my work. Don't *you*, Professor?'

'Oh, I do indeed,' Dobie admitted. 'In fact, many people form the impression that I'm a little absent-minded.'

'A misleading impression, I'm sure. Spread by the Christian dogmatists, perhaps.'

'And perhaps misleading in your case, too. I suppose you wouldn't care, er...to sign a confession?'

'... But that's *ridiculous!*' Jackson said.

'The trouble is,' Dobie said, sighing heavily, 'that you and Dancey are really two of a kind. He, it would seem, has very little historical imagination and *you*, if I may say so, have very little grasp of the most elementary principles of mathematics. Such as the laws of symmetry.'

'Well, that's where you're wrong. I've had *some* training as a police officer, you know. First of all, it isn't true you have to be six feet under. That's a popular phallus, that is. Four foot six, that's what the law says. Though what that's got to do—'

'Jackson.'

'Yes?'

'We do have difficulty, don't we, in understanding one another at times. It must be the generation gap or something. Let me begin at the beginning. You must understand that Third Class students—and Dancey is such a student, if ever I saw one—very rarely cheat. They are modest. They are humble. They are resigned to their lot. Besides, they have very little to gain by doing so. Students of First Class potential are, as the classification would suggest, in an altogether different category. They are ambitious. They are subject to all kinds of external pressure and psychological strain. They'll cheat like anything if you give them half a chance. And Freda Hearne is one such—if I mistake not, Jackson.'

'Ah. Well, I think I follow that. Only thing is, I'm here about the murder, so to speak. So unless there's some kind of a connection—'

Dobie clicked his tongue. 'But there is, there is. That's why she killed him. I don't know exactly what Croaker had in the way of proof—'

'And I don't know what *you* can have in the way of proof. The whole idea's... It's what I said. Ridiculous. How could a little slip of a girl stab a man with a thing like *this?*' Jackson grabbed the sword and swung it vigorously to and fro. 'It's *heavy*. She wouldn't be strong enough. Even assuming she had the thing in the first place, which she didn't have, because Dancey had, I mean Dancey... *Whooooops.* Sorry.'

'That's all right. Croaker won't be using that inkwell any more, in any case. Rather garish effect, though, isn't it? All that red ink alongside the... Ah well. Never mind. He was using it earlier this morning, that's the point. I mean, here it is. He's written it down. Plain as the nose on your face, if you'll excuse a personal comment.'

Jackson put down the sword and stared at the topmost sheet of paper on the table. 'NOT *a Roman sword—a spearhead.* But that's just a *correction*, something he's written on a student's essay...'

'Dancey's essay, in fact. A little ironic touch, that, which the Emperor Julian himself might have appreciated.' Dobie moved over to the glass collection cabinet and lifted the lid. 'There's the implement in question. An authentic Roman spearhead. A long, thin point, as you see, something like a modern javelin. She'll have wiped it, of course. No prints. But your people should be able to turn up some residual blood and tissue without too much trouble. It was essentially an *easy* murder, you see. She just went round behind him towards the bookshelves, opened the cabinet, turned round again and—*whack.*'

Jackson winced. 'But, but... But...'

'Wiped the thing on his coat—put it back in the cabinet—grabbed the book that was her planned excuse for going into the study at all and walked out the door with it. Twenty seconds or less from start to finish. But, of course, it was always obvious Croaker hadn't been stabbed with a sword. There's too much blood for that. If a sword's left in the wound, the opening's virtually sealed. It only bleeds like that when you pull it out. Which is what she did when she removed the spearhead.'

'But the sword *was* in the wound. I saw it. We all did.'

'Dancey didn't. He couldn't have, since

it was in his hand at the time. But then, he says, he put it down on the table and hurried off to inform Copleston, and then he and Copleston phoned the ambulance and the police. But the telephone—as you'll have noticed when you used it yourself—is in that recess behind the door.'

'That's right. You can't see the door to the study, you have your back turned to it anyway when you're using the telephone—'

'And no doubt they'd both have been pretty engrossed, as Freda Hearne would put it, in talking to the hospital and the police. For at least a couple of minutes, maybe three or four, in which time of course the girl could slip back into the study and arrange, in effect, her own alibi. I agree she mightn't have been strong enough to transfix a *living* man with a sword, but pushing down on a *dead* man with all her weight...she wouldn't even have had to touch the hilt and wouldn't have wanted to in any case, as she knew Dancey's fingerprints would certainly be on it. And going into the original entry wound, the sword blade would eventually mask it completely, being much wider and thicker than the spearhead. Neat but not gaudy, as the monkey said—'

'But how did she *know* about it? That business with Dancey and the sword? She didn't see it. She was sitting out there in the library at the time.'

'Copleston told her about it. At least...we know he told *someone* about it because he said so. And he couldn't have commented on it to anyone else because there wasn't anyone else in the library at that time.'

'Well, damn it,' Jackson said. 'Who'd've thought it? A nice young lady like that.'

'*I* thought it,' Dobie said immodestly, 'as soon as I saw which book she'd borrowed. Being myself a mathematician, you see, I was able immediately to grasp the difference between two and three.'

'Between two and three...what?' Jackson was getting befuddled.

'Well, she must have grabbed for it in a bit too much of a hurry. Which is understandable. But as you can see, there are three identically-bound volumes... She got the wrong one, that's all. Volume Two instead of Volume Three. And being eighteenth-century editions, they're properly indexed. The references to Julian she was citing are all in the sixth treatise, that's Volume Three. So she must have borrowed Volume Three earlier and copied them all down then. She couldn't have been copying them this morning or she'd have realised her mistake.'

'You mean that was her cover story, like? So she could be seen to be working in the library until the boy came back and she could work the switch?'

'Exactly. Well, that's another of the marks of a First Class mind, Jacko. Thorough preparation. But once in a while...a little *too* thorough. Oh, and I shouldn't worry about the Rector, if I were you. Freda Hearne may have a First Class mind but *he* hasn't. Just tell him you've made an arrest and leave it at that.'

Body Language

Clare Curzon

'Brandy Balls,' muttered the blonde.

Startled, Farringdon contemplated the bottle of Grand Marnier beside him as though it might suddenly prove capable of animal functions.

'And wine gums,' the girl regretted. 'Smuggled into the dorm for midnight orgies. We were determined to get tight.'

He smiled benignly. 'You must have been very young.'

She became ruefully aware of having spoken aloud. 'So young that we *did* get tight, just from wishing.' She sank her vodka Martini. 'Now it's harder.'

Extended on the lounger beside the pool bar, her cutaway bikini revealing the harsh pelvic angles, the stretched, sinewy hollows at the jointing of oiled, lightly roasted limbs, she reminded him of a succulent cold chicken carcase, meant to be pulled apart and eaten with the fingers, soft inner

71

flesh white and faintly stained at the edges with pink. He could even taste her, greasy and slightly salted, with a lingering Ambre Solaire bitterness on the lips.

She closed her eyes, done with him as passive audience. Farringdon swung back to the counter, raising an eyebrow at the barman who consolingly pushed a pottery dish of assorted nuts towards him.

Across the horseshoe bar two English boys, still pale shrimp pink, were counting out unfamiliar coins, uncertain of the array of bottles on offer. Beginners.

Farringdon glanced down the tanned length of his own muscled arm to the glass grasped in the cardplayer's fingers. An Old Hand, he assessed himself drily, and smiled.

Abandoning all pretence of rest, the blonde swung her legs down, kicked on her espadrilles and walked stiff-legged away, dragging her gaudy beach towel.

Impetuous, Farringdon decided. Passionate, perhaps even desperate. Something wrong there. He sensed a story in her.

The Spanish barman came back, met his eyes, refilled his coffee cup alongside the empty glass. 'A regular?' Farringdon asked.

'She come three years now. 'as a month

timeshare with 'er 'usband. This year—she is a widow, she tell me.'

'So she came alone?' What was that—daring, rebellious, nostalgic? Maybe all three.

'Alone, no. She bring another lady.'

'Ah.' Farringdon slowly finished his drink, slid from the stool, smoothed his hands along the dark wings of hair, and barefoot made his rippling way back along the pool side to the company office. The woman interested him. One of last night's arrivals, she retained suntan from a previous time abroad. Anyone using a sun-bed would have made a more decisive effort.

Expressionlessly the barman watched his big-cat progress to check on the woman whose story he'd hinted at. Security, the man's function was called. How secure would anyone be, crossing the path of such a one?

Farringdon sweethearted the office girl to give him computer time. He tapped in his code and brought up the timeshare registrations for three years back, monthly purchases commencing mid-May. Three couples' names came up; Frewen, Crosby and Lambton. He pressed EXIT and tapped in Frewen, but the ages were twenty years out.

The Crosbys, he found, had three children and lived in Northampton. He couldn't see the blonde with that background. Lambton, then.

Yes. Lambton, Hendrik, Chairman of a shipping company registered in Hong Kong, resident London. Sounded Anglo-Dutch, wealthy too. Earlier trips to the Far East could account for the wife's established suntan; Memsahib with parasol. And Madam was a widow. So where was the woman companion she'd brought along?

The question was answered as they sat together at dinner, blonde and black hair bent over their seafood cocktails. The brunette had a glossy, tight-curled coiffure fresh from the company hairdressing salon.

She was the very antithesis of the Widow Lambton, within the limits of female kind: plump against the other's leanness, excited against the other's ennui. And while one seemed oblivious to all around, she was playing Look-at-Me, the large, dark eyes wide, the fleshy little body thrusting itself from a zebra confection of magenta and white see-through tulle.

When a table adjoining theirs became free, Farringdon went across to claim it, a discreet snap of the fingers sending the *maître d'* to head off a couple waiting by the door. He seated himself facing the girl companion, the blonde in profile. Panning his gaze casually around the restaurant he let it rest a moment on the magenta stripes, travel slowly up and meet eyes alive for the encounter. And he smiled, making the slightest lifting of his glass in her direction. Then his eyes moved on, came to rest on the menu which the waiter leaned in to present.

He lingered over his meal with selective enjoyment, never meeting the eager gaze again. It was enough. Contact was made. The rest would follow in good time.

From behind the venetian blinds of his eyrie suite he later watched couples dancing on the terrace below, some close-held, others wildly gyrating, head-tossing, alone. Reluctantly the blonde had joined the other girl, languidly making the routine steps, then, as the rhythm got to her, flinging her limbs in jerky, neurotic movements, snatching them back before their full release.

The body language of torment, Farringdon thought and was unsurprised when suddenly she broke away, calling back over her shoulder to the plump, dark girl who stood deserted among the surging bodies of the other dancers.

But she was alone only a moment. One of the English boys of the pool bar seized her hand and she was swung back into the youthful frenzy.

Farringdon stroked his chin thoughtfully. Give it half an hour, then he'd call at Mrs Lambton's apartment to return the lace shawl she'd left in the restaurant. Meanwhile the English daily papers had arrived from the airport. He had time enough to scan the headlines.

It took him longer than intended because on the *Telegraph's* Home News page, spread across a double column, was Davina Lambton's face, with inset a smaller picture of a thin-faced older man. 'Heiress Denies Husband's Suicide Threat,' screamed the headline.

So Farringdon read the whole thing through, and was better armed when he went ringing at the doorbell of Apartment 108.

The door opened suddenly on to a dark

interior and an imperative *'sh!'*

He eased in like a conspirator, aware that silhouetted against the light from the Andalucian lamp on the patio wall he would have been unrecognisable. It would be a shock when she discovered who had been let in.

But the real shock was his.

He followed her through the darkened hall, past a closed bedroom door, into the kitchen and living area, all unlit, to arrive on the rear patio ablaze with lights. The girl turned and gasped, 'Oh, it's *you!*'

But it was the wrong woman. The companion must have quickly abandoned the dance scene and come back to find Davina retired to bed. Perhaps she'd hoped the English boy would follow.

'I—' Farringdon began, proffering the wispy shawl.

'Oh, thanks. It's my—it's my friend's.'

No, Farringdon decided. The word she'd been going to say was 'boss's'. Only that relationship would account for her rapid return when she was out for a good time. She wasn't the naturally protective type.

'Is Mrs Lambton sleeping?' he asked, exploring cautiously.

'Deep under,' said the girl, with a wide

grin. 'Make yourself cosy.' She indicated cushioned loungers side by side under the purple bougainvillea.

This was one of the best ground-floor apartments of the development, with not only a terrace but a path of grey volcanic grit leading through a small garden with three young banana trees and a tall flowering cactus to a low white wall. Beyond this ran the stream which later dropped some sixteen feet in a cataract that was the central feature of the 'village' garden. Overall there was a rich, heady scent of well-watered vegetation and perfumed flowers.

'I'll fetch the drinks trolley. I was just restocking it,' the girl said and moved back to the kitchen area.

Farringdon shook up the cushions and eased himself on to the nearer lounger, then swung his feet back to sit wide-kneed at right angles in the centre. Relaxation wasn't the message to put across. Faced with the wrong woman, he was for once uncertain how to proceed.

Wheeling the drinks trolley out, the girl suddenly stopped at the terrace edge and gave a low gasp. She sprang at Farringdon, kicking his legs off the ground, backing off something small that approached over the marble tiles.

The creature scuttled rapidly towards her, tail stiffly high in a menacing arc. She slid off a sandal, bent swiftly and dealt it a death blow. Then several more to register her loathing, and a dark liquid stained the tiles. Then with the sandal's tip she dribbled its carcase to the edge of the grit path. Its shell lay stiff and shiny, still in the posture of attack, still recognisably what it had so lately been.

Sobered by the speed of her reaction, Farringdon reflected that—though it could signify nothing—his own birth sign was the Scorpion.

He thanked her nicely for the rescue and the Martini, and departed swift upon it. It had always suited him best to be the knight-at-arms and not the distressed damsel. Besides, he felt a need to ponder, and to make a call to England to an old acquaintance in the Met.

Next morning dawned, as it ever seemed to in the Canaries, with a promise of golden sunshine tempered by island breezes. Farringdon swam early and dried off by the pool, lazily amused by the antics of a young family alongside. The younger child, a girl of three, was revelling in the freedom of no clothes. Her old brother was constrained by Mother to retain his bathing trunks.

'*You* can't take *your* swimsuit off,' the little girl accused. 'You've got *bits!*'

A worthy recruit for the monstrous regiment of women, Farringdon noted. Which returned his thoughts to the two women lately arrived in Apartment 108. With luck there should be something on them faxed through for him by noon.

From the office window two hours later he observed the blonde arrive in a one-piece swimsuit, deposit her towel by the edge of the pool, walk to where the water was deepest and dive neatly in. The companion's actions—settling herself with reading matter, sun specs and beach bag alongside their shared property, confirmed his earlier estimate of her function. She was there to mind things, stay in the background and keep off unwanted attentions. Secretary, nurse or warder, though? Certainly something more formidable than the naîve role she'd been playing in the restaurant.

If, new to High Life, she'd really been eager for paperback romance, would she so easily have accepted his early departure last night? And that scorpion incident—it had betrayed her. Not only was she familiar with sub-tropical hazards, but she'd revealed her own rapid reactions, a ruthless purpose and a total lack of squeamish femininity. Jen Franks, as she had introduced herself last night, was not at all what at first she seemed.

The information from London came as a person-to-person call. Chief Inspector Meredith, CID, was delighted to learn the whereabouts of the Widow Lambton, the more so since she had vanished before it was possible to warn her not to leave the country. No travel tickets or hotel bookings for that name had been issued through the principal London agencies. Regrettably the Met had been unaware of the late Mr Hendrik Lambton's Canaries timeshare.

As to Jen Franks, the name rang no bell, but the description matched an unidentified female companion seen with the dead man during his last weeks. Although of European appearance she was thought to have Far East connections. And yes, the widow had stood to inherit from her husband's apparent suicide. Her declaration that he would never kill himself could be double bluff, because the scientific experts were now coming up with some clear indications that the late gentleman had been hastened on his way by a third party with access to heroin.

'Get me a name for the oriental lady,' Farringdon insisted. 'I'll ring you at 8.00 pm. Can you have it by then?'

'I don't see why not,' said Meredith urbanely. 'Keep an eye on the widow till we can send someone out to talk to her.'

Mrs Lambton had booked a session with the club masseuse after siesta that afternoon, which should leave her companion free for whatever role she fancied. Farringdon kept watch, assigning more routine matters—two complaints of missing property and one of sexual harassment by a geriatric man—to his assistant.

When the pool was almost deserted after lunch the plump dark girl reappeared in beach dungarees and set up camp on a lounger. Farringdon took a tray with two long drinks to join her. She started playing Poor Little Me All Alone, and he kept to the game's rules, even teasing her into the shallows for a boisterous round of splashing. Back on the pool side she slid under her umbrella. He had to coax her out for a coating of protective oil. From the beach bag. And groping there, he felt in an inside pocket the hard outline of a passport, wallet and cheque book.

Eventually, after further plying with soft drinks, she withdrew, coyly remarking on the need to repair her face. He lay back, eyes closed, and the fool girl dipped in the bag for her vanity case, leaving him all the rest.

Supple fingers on a trailing arm effected all he required. Yawning, he turned on his side and scanned the opened passport. When the girl returned he seemed quite genuinely asleep, seraphically smiling since he was now ahead of London's Met.

The masseuse reported on the widow, standing behind him as he sat and firmly thumbing his cervical vertebrae, partly from pleasure and partly from habit. 'Very tense,' she pronounced. 'Had a quiet little weep when I got her loosened up. Not that I let on I noticed, of course.'

'Fear, remorse or plain guilt?' he wondered aloud.

The wise woman offered no opinion. He moved off to other duties, different subjects for his probing. At 8.00 pm he dialled Meredith in London and discovered they had the same name for the widow's companion.

'Slack of your lot not to check all passports on arrival,' grunted the Met man.

'It's not a custom I intend to alter. Our permanent staff know the timeshare owners, who are responsible for their guests. It's a club here after all. How did Mrs Lambton come to employ the girl?'

'Rang an agency for a secretary-companion. They sent two applicants who weren't suitable, and someone in Lambton's London office recommended "Jen Franks". We're looking into the man's background.'

'So what's *her* background?'

'An adopted orphan. We're waiting for full details from the Hong Kong police.'

From the plane, coming in to land next evening, the south side of the island appeared dull brown and black. Meredith marvelled that anyone should choose to holiday at a volcanic desert. And then, transported by cab to the luxurious oasis of the development, he was overwhelmed by the voluptuous beauty of bougainvilleas, oleanders and hibiscus in purple, flame, peach, and gold.

Sweating in his summer suit he was shown to his Grade A apartment, to reappear anonymously in lycra trunks, accompanied by his junior in jailbird-striped Bermuda shorts. Farringdon insisted on their pool baptism before the serious business of haute cuisine.

'The case is neatly tied up. Only the arrest remains,' Meredith purred, settling at ease with his after-dinner cigar. 'But what first spiked your interest?'

'Take people's clothes off,' Farringdon said urbanely, 'and body language speaks out loud. The widow was a victim running for cover, and cover for her was somewhere she could lie low and lick her wounds. The other one was a greedy child offered a plate of goodies, wanting them all and at any cost: eager to come into her own and not too sure what to snatch first.

'Either she had expectations, with a blackmailer's hold over her employer, or a direct line to instant success. I preferred the latter option.

'The widow would no longer be the beneficiary of her husband's will if she was

85

proved to have killed him. And you were investigating her already. So with Davina eliminated, who was next in line? It had to be a relative: since he'd no official family, then a natural child who could prove its parentage.

'When "Jen Franks" and her London accomplice had perfected the watertight proof of Davina's guilt, the girl would have returned to Hong Kong, and while the law dallied over disposal of Lambton's fortune she would have had time to become once more the Rose Lamb Koo she was registered as at birth.

'By the time she arrived in England to claim her inheritance in person she would have been unrecognisable to anyone acquainted with Jen Franks.'

Meredith frowned at him. 'Not that corny old "Master of Disguises" stuff?'

'No. But in features she happens to resemble her dead father, a fair, thin man. So, as well as dyeing her hair, wearing tinted lenses and cheek pads, she had silicon implants. Not just where most women prefer them, but on thighs, arms, shoulders, to make a thin girl into a fatty.

'Who would suspect a personable young

woman of choosing to look like a balloon? But implants can also be surgically re-moved, leaving only temporary scarring. No-one in London would remember Jen Franks when they later met Lambton's illegitimate daughter. And the widow, who had spent most time with her, would be languishing in jail.

'As I said, remove people's clothes and the body language comes over loud. Get a chance actually to touch them and the message can be deafening. The last clue came during our horseplay in the pool. Under her dungarees she was wearing an inflated bodice.'

'Wouldn't you know,' Meredith inquired of the stars through his rising smoke rings, 'that while I do the donkey work, Farringdon gets a job where he's paid to finger the ladies?'

The Bottle Dungeon

Antonia Fraser

'Quite rare nowadays, I believe,' said Joss Benmuir, looking down beyond his feet at the black hole.

'It may be quite rare but it's absolutely horrible! Really, Joss, I fail to see how you can—' Lady Martin paused, then went on with fervour '—*tolerate* something so totally *foul.*'

'It's not a human rights issue, Aunt May, at least not now.' The intention of Robbie Benmuir was evidently to tease. May Martin was an extremely wealthy widow: since her husband's death she had occupied herself as an indefatigable campaigner for every conceivable liberal issue. Her figure was a familiar one, holding up a sandwich board of protest, spread across some newspaper.

Jemima Shore shivered as she too looked down. The Bottle Dungeon was carved—literally—out of rock. It consisted of a long narrow 'neck' which bellied out into a circular 'bottle', the shape of which could not be discerned from above until Joss Benmuir swung his flashlight into its depths. There were no steps cut in the 'neck'. The only method of getting down (or up) consisted of using a thick rope, currently coiled beside them, and fastened to an enormous iron ring in the stone.

Privately Jemima agreed with Lady Martin that there was something foul about the gaping hole. She also fancied that there was a fetid smell. No light, not much air and absolutely no sanitation beyond a tiny aperture in the rock at the bottom of the bottle which dropped to the sea—no wonder there was something dank and rotten in the atmosphere of the stone cell which contained the entrance to the dungeon. But since Jemima was an outsider at this house party, she decided to stay silent. She had been working with May Martin in recent months on a project for a television series tentatively entitled 'A woman's right to say anything' (the female political voice in various totalitarian countries). She had become fond of the old lady, faintly ridiculous in her untidy appearance, certainly often ridiculed in the Press for her views; yet ever gallant in her defence of those unable to speak for themselves. When her own New Year plans fell through, she had accepted Lady Martin's invitation to be her companion on the Scottish trip.

'Not really a party,' Lady Martin had pronounced, 'in spite of its being Hogmanay. There aren't any neighbours for miles. Plenty of time to work together.' She hesitated. 'Thank heaven you're not married; you'll take Joss's mind off that dreadful Clio Brown; then of course there's Robbie.'

A slightly uncomfortable silence followed Robbie Benmuir's little sally about human rights. To May Martin at least such matters were not a laughing matter. It was broken by Joss, who continued to gaze down into the dungeon as he spoke. 'It's a tourist attraction, Aunt May. That's what it is. And a very fine one, too. After all, who else would come to this desolate spot otherwise? So many finer castles, aren't there? And you know how I need the money.' His tone was perfectly equable; nevertheless the words only increased the general embarrassment. Joss was being deliberately provocative: as Jemima Shore already knew enough about the Benmuir family set-up to appreciate.

May Martin was probably rich enough to restore the crumbling castle (what remained of it) single-handed, but preferred to spend her money on good causes—which did not include Castle Crask. And there was nothing to stop her doing so. Although Joss and Robbie, the children of her late brother, were her only blood relations, May Martin's money came entirely from the man she had married comparatively late in her life and very late in his, Sir Ludwig Martin, founder of LudMart. She had confided to Jemima on the way up: 'Joss wants me to "invest" in Crask—his phrase. He should know by now that I only make strictly philanthropic investments, which does not include ancient masonry, even if it is owned by my family.'

As if there weren't enough tensions within the party already, thought Jemima. What with Clio Brown being once upon a time a girlfriend of Robbie. Clio Brown and her overweight and overanxious husband, Gerald (why on earth had she married him? The answer was, presumably, money) and now apparently—all too apparently this afternoon—Clio Brown and Joss. Jemima Shore had taken a strong dislike to Clio

Brown. She hoped it was not jealousy on her part. Clio, with her cat's face and fashionably cropped dark hair, so tall, so slim and at the same time so curved, was certainly amazingly good-looking. But there was something intensely disagreeable about her. Gerald bore the brunt of her bad moods: the sight of his red, perspiring face—even in the un-centrally-heated castle he seemed perpetually hot—would remind Clio that she needed a handkerchief fetching from her bedroom. She seemed to take a malevolent pleasure in watching Gerald trying to fit his bulk up a curved stone staircase.

Joss Benmuir was right: Crask was indeed a desolate spot, situated on a headland which ran out into the North Sea where even the harsh cries of the sea birds seemed to have something lonely and despairing about them. It had not always been so. Crask's moat was now dry, but its depth indicated that the castle had once acted as an important fortress, ready to repel foreign raiders and hand-off domestic assailants with equal ferocity. Its strategic position meant that some kind of defensive structure must always have existed on the site—there were even traces of a prehistoric *dun*—but the present castle had been predominantly built in the fourteenth century. It had however been badly battered during the Cromwellian invasion of Scotland and suffered again in the period of the Jacobite risings.

As Colonel Benmuir, father of Joss and Robbie, had been wont to lament: 'It's centuries since we Benmuirs managed to find ourselves on the winning side.' He sometimes added: 'Perhaps that's where poor May gets her taste for losers from—the spirit of her ancestors.'

Two substantial towers did however remain of the fourteenth century castle: but they were no longer joined by a great hall or other buildings. The space in between was occupied by grass and stones, some of which were big enough to cause unwary guests to stumble as they moved between the two separate structures which together made up the living quarters of the modern Benmuir family. There was no protection on the headland—mountains existed only in the distance—and the gusts of wind carried the sea spray inland and had been known to whirl umbrellas away: that had happened to Jemima Shore on the previous evening, so that her beautiful crushed velvet skirt had become sodden. Now, as they stood outside, a girl called Ellie MacSomething—attached to Robbie it seemed—who had suffered similarly with her tartan wool skirt, was bold enough to ask Joss why there was no covered way.

'It would blow away like your umbrella,' Joss remarked blandly. 'Wouldn't it, Robbie? At least you didn't stumble over a sheep: my father used to keep sheep here to deal with the grass. I got rid of them. Besides, we chaps like leading our own lives. Robbie has always got a home here. Until I marry, that is.'

'And will you and your wife have separate towers when you marry?' There was something provocative about the way Ellie MacSomething was pursuing the matter and it occurred to Jemima that she might be thinking of transferring her affections from Robbie to his elder brother. Joss, with his pale face, the black hair falling romantically over the eyes with their heavy lids, had more the air of a Spanish grandee—an El Greco—than a Scot. Robbie on the other hand, with his rosy, almost ruddy cheeks, his freckles, his brownish curly hair already slipping back on his forehead, with stocky figure was the same physical type as his aunt May. Although Jemima had the impression of intelligence beneath Robbie's jokey manner, there was no doubt which brother was the better-looking and Joss was after all the owner of Crask (whatever that might mean).

'Separate towers for married couples! What a good idea!' said Clio Brown suddenly. 'Gerald, I think we should get on much better like that. Towers with thick walls. Too thick for even your snores to penetrate.' She smiled in her peculiar cat-like manner, the corners of her small, perfectly bowed mouth, turning up as though she was contemplating a small mouse before her. The mouse however was her large husband. One could not say that Gerald Brown flushed, since his face was red enough already, nevertheless it was clear that the remark had wounded him—but then that was presumably the intention.

By unspoken agreement, the other guests turned back to their contemplation of the Bottle Dungeon. They had all been taken on a visit to Crask's famous attraction—if a dungeon could really be so described—as a post-lunch treat by their host. The light faded early on a midwinter Scottish afternoon and as Joss Benmuir jocularly observed: 'We don't want to lose one of you down the neck, not on the eve of Hogmanay anyway, it might ruin our modest celebrations.'

He touched the aperture with his toe. 'There's one at St Andrew's Castle but ours is a whole foot deeper. Twenty six foot deep.'

Jemima shivered again. She still could not easily bear to contemplate the idea of a prisoner being lowered into the depths and left—left without light, heat, food beyond what the captors condescended to lower, left in the filth, a prey to rats...for there were apparently rats there in the past, probably introduced down the neck by the jailers, since the drainage hole at the bottom was minute, too small for a mouse to enter let alone a rat...

In desperation Jemima found herself asking, 'Did anyone ever escape?' It was the best she could do to strike a more cheerful note. Before Joss could answer, May Martin said, very fiercely indeed: 'The terrible thing is that people *lived*, not that they died. Death was *merciful* compared to what people endured down there. Sometimes for years. An amazing aspect of the human spirit: some people are survivors. Joss, I really think you should seal it off, not exhibit it, show some respect for the sufferings of human beings...'

Fortunately for Joss he was able to ignore his aunt in favour of answering Jemima. 'No-one escaped.' He pointed to some lettering cut in the side of the stone cell. *Initus non abeat.* Mediaeval Latin. It means: once in, you can't get out. Carved shortly after the castle was built, they think.' Joss paused. 'No-one escaped without help, that is. Some prisoner, put down there for supporting John Knox, at the time of the Reformation, that sort of thing, did get out. But it turned out that the jailer's daughter had helped him out with a rope. Otherwise: *Initus non abeat.* That's a bottle dungeon for you.'

'Just like marriage,' said Clio Brown suddenly. 'Once in, there's no way out. Unless you get help.' At first the company assumed that this was merely one of Clio's unpleasant interjections intended primarily to bait her husband. But it turned out that she had more to say. 'I want to go down, Joss. I want to see what it's like.

It could be quite an experience. I want to spend the night down there. It should be'—she lifted her lips in her little cat's smile again—'gloriously private. Look how narrow that neck is. Gerald, I don't believe you could fit down there, even if the rope would hold you.'

There was polite laughter from those like Ellie and Jemima who decided to pretend that Clio was joking. Gerald merely spluttered; but this time there was no doubt at all in Jemima's mind that he was seriously angry, and Clio might find she had gone for once a little too far. She did not however act as if she was aware of her husband's rage. On the contrary, she persisted in talking about her descent, cajoled Joss into revealing that there was a rope ladder for emergencies, narrow but serviceable, in a locked cupboard in the corner of the cell and finally provoked Gerald into shouting at her:

'If that's how you want to see the New Year in, God damn it, don't count on finding me in a very good mood tomorrow morning.'

'I don't count on finding you at all tomorrow morning, Gerald, if you go on shouting like this,' replied Clio smoothly.

'You're straining yourself dreadfully with all that shouting, and you know what the doctor said. Rage is not healthful.' Clio sounded so primly reproachful that you might almost have thought that the previous scene in which she deliberately provoked her husband's anger had not taken place.

'And wouldn't you be pleased?' snarled Gerald. 'A rich widow. Well, don't count on that either.'

The embarrassment continued.

Afterwards it became important as to who had first suggested the bet. Was it Joss, his black eyes as he challenged Clio in a way that seemed positively sexual even at the comparatively asexual hour of three o'clock in the afternoon? Or perhaps frivolous, giggly Ellie, seeking to stir up further trouble? Or the much calmer and more self-possessed Robbie, with exactly the opposite aim of defusing the situation? Jemima had certainly not done so—she continued to regard the Bottle Dungeon with revulsion—while Lady Martin made her indignation quite obvious.

'Sensation-monger!' she said to Jemima in an aside which was clearly intended to be heard. 'The sort of person who collects

Nazi mementos for kicks.'

Gerald had been the first one actually to use the word 'bet'.

'I bet you won't stay down there for one hour, Clio, let alone for one night.' Then he stumped away from the party, with the words: 'Do what you damn well please! You always do.' But it was after that the real bet somehow evolved: the bet that Clio would be lowered down by the little ladder, as warmly clad as possible, plus sleeping-bag and flashlight, and a pocket heater, generally used out shooting, to warm her hands. This lowering would take place at eleven o'clock that night. She would be formally let out—let up—one hour later, with the New Year.

'And what does she get if she wins the bet?' asked Ellie, who had gone back to twining herself round Robbie again.

'I get to choose how I spend the rest of the night.' Jemima swore that Clio actually licked her lips when she said that, certainly there was a flicker of her little red tongue as she smiled. 'Which means,' she went on, looking at each of the three men in turn, ending with her husband: 'I get to spend it alone.'

It was not until dinner, when all had

changed including Clio who wore a black lycra cat-suit, that Robbie made the obvious point.

'I've just realised she's bound to win the bet, isn't she? Unless she dies of fright or something awful like that. You see if Clio does want to come up—come up early and lose the bet—she has no way of letting us know, has she? She just has to sit it out down there—yuk—until we come and get her. Next year.'

So it was agreed that Clio should be installed with a large noisy bell, which Robbie found, once used to summon labourers for lunch. If the bell was heard to ring, it would be regarded as a sign that Clio needed help and the bet was off.

'Send not to know for whom the bell tolls,'—Robbie being jokey again—'because it will definitely be Clio. After all, once in you can't get out. Without help. Good family motto that, Joss, we should use it. After all we Benmuirs are always getting into things we can't get out of, aren't we: relationships, debt, that sort of thing.' Lady Martin and Joss both frowned.

The presence of the bell meant that the door to the stone cell had to be left open: Robbie was not sure the clang from the depths would otherwise be heard. But no-one felt that to be a problem. The door was clearly visible across the rough grass from the Big Tower where the party was congregated in the big sitting room on the first floor, also used as a dining room on festive occasions, with its high windows and seats in the embrasures. Nobody could rescue Clio early—supposing anyone was minded to do so—without being observed.

'Not even to drop down the teeniest reviving malt whisky,' Robbie, determinedly light-hearted again. But none of the badinage was really very light-hearted. Something—what exactly and when?—had gone too far. A trouble-making young woman, a stupid bet, what a recipe for New Year's Eve! (Jemima Shore wished she were at home, celebrating with her cat, appropriately named Midnight).

About ten-thirty both Gerald Brown and Lady Martin decided to opt out of the proceedings—including the seeing-in of the New Year—and went to their respective beds. The Browns were sleeping in the Little Tower, or Robbie's Tower, together with Ellie and Robbie himself; Lady Martin and Jemima were housed still higher up in the Big Tower. Joss as host, now politely insisted on escorting Lady Martin upstairs, despite her protests about knowing the way perfectly well.

'But Joss, I grew up here!' she exclaimed. Perhaps he intended to make his touch at this point, thought Jemima, although it was scarcely a tactful moment with her disapproval so manifest. Gerald's bulky figure could be seen crossing the grass, bending slightly as he fronted the wind. The moon, almost full, had now risen, and with its eerie glow on the stones, did something to supplement the inadequate lighting of the passage between the two towers.

After a short while Clio said crossly, 'I hope he hasn't gone to sleep already. I've got to put a great many things over this.' She stretched out in her skin-tight black suit: she really did have the most beautiful lissome figure, small high breasts clearly visible under the lycra, and the narrow thighs and long, long legs of a model; she actually could wear her cat-suit and get away with it. 'I'll be back,' said Clio. 'May he not be *snoring*, that's all I ask.'

A few moments later they watched Clio in her turn cross the grass, a cumbersome parka over her cat-suit, as the winds tossed her short hair. Whatever passed between the Browns on the first floor of the Little Tower must however have been vaguely conciliatory because they saw Gerald at the window, raising his hand and waving. His mood must have improved since he left. Clio reappeared shortly afterwards.

'Of course he's in a better temper!' she exclaimed. 'He just thinks I'll lose, that's why. He's really a cunning old sod, that one. Convinced I'll panic and ring the bell. Such a downer. I really can't think why I married him.' Jemima, looking at her, now more of a Michelin woman in her jerseys, thought: why did he marry you? Do some men just like to be humiliated? Answer, I suppose: yes.

In the event, the actual descent of Clio on the rope ladder was a slight anti-climax. Her sleek head had disappeared from view into the Bottle Dungeon without anything more dramatic happening than her own voice echoing upwards: 'It's great down here, the new holiday spot, can't think why those prisoners complained.'

'Any rats?' called Robbie.

'They're all upstairs,' Clio shouted back. 'Or asleep.' She was in her usual form. The flashlight was seen to cast its sepulchral glow upwards, the bell was tested (it sounded very loud) and then there was nothing to do but brave the wind and go back to the Big Tower again and wait.

There nobody could quite think how to fill in the time. The general clear view of the open door of the cell meant that it was impossible to forget Clio. Joss, their host, had fallen moodily silent, his thoughts no doubt with her. The hour looked like passing slowly until Robbie decided to organise them.

'Here we are, four people in search of an occupation. Is it to be a foursome reel or bridge?'

Although Ellie clapped her hands and voted for a reel, Jemima hastily pointed out she did not know how to dance a reel. So they all four settled for bridge. After that the time did pass a little quicker although the fact that the bridge table was placed in the embrasure containing the big window meant that the Bottle Dungeon—and Clio—remained somewhere in Jemima's thoughts at least. Nor did the bridge prove quite the engrossing occupation for herself and Ellie they might have anticipated. The Benmuir brothers, Joss playing with

Jemima, and Robbie with Ellie, played virtually every hand themselves, bidding, it seemed, with the aim of so doing. The one hand Jemima did play, Joss peered over her shoulder silently, but somehow, she felt, critically. Ellie never got to play a single hand.

It was actually Robbie who was busy making six spades—his luck was in—when they heard the bell ring. It rang loudly, the sound melted away into the wind, then it rang again. Instinctively Jemima looked at her watch: it was ten minutes to twelve. The others simply jumped up; then all of them started to run down the twisting stair, Joss pushing open the door, and out across the moonlit grass. Ellie stumbled twice but Robbie did not stop to help her. The brothers reached the cell together, leading Jemima herself by at least fifteen yards. By the time she arrived, the rope ladder was already being lowered and Joss was speaking soothing words to Clio—soothing and openly tender. But then Gerald was not present.

'Now then, darling, it's going to be all right. Trust Joss. Easy goes. Come on, my beautiful darling.'

And after a few moments, Clio's head

emerged once again: but it was a very different Clio, tear-stained, dirty—filthy dirty—and more or less incoherent. Jemima felt no particular pleasure at the sight; as a matter of fact she found she preferred the confident if disagreeable Clio to this pathetic victim. Finally, how little Clio had known herself! She had been so sure of her own nerves, and so absolutely wrong when it came to the crunch. 'The shadows, the ghosts of the prisoners trying to kill me,' were some of the things Clio babbled about. At least Lady Martin might have been pleased at this last-minute sensitivity to the sufferings of people in the past. Still hysterical, Clio was led away in the direction of the Little Tower; it was now Robbie, not Joss, who took her arm, as though in tacit agreement that the Little Tower was 'Robbie's.' Joss, Ellie and Jemima trailed after them.

'Nobody ever asked what would happen if she lost the bet!' cried Ellie suddenly: Jemima guessed she was annoyed at Robbie's attention to Clio.

'She gets to spend the night with Gerald,' snapped Joss, evidently made equally tense by the sight of Robbie's arm round Clio. Ellie continued to gaze after them.

108

'My room is on the ground floor, overlooking the sea,' she said, 'I suppose I'd better go to it. It must be midnight by now. Happy New Year.' Ellie did not even try to sound sincere. The door above their heads opened and shut; immediately Robbie came clattering back down the stairs; Clio had been tactfully left to face Gerald—if awake—by herself. Ellie was therefore looking slightly happier when Clio started to scream for the second time that night. This time there were no sobs, just sheer horror. What Clio was screaming over and over again, as she half ran, half fell down the stairway till she reached Robbie (and Joss) was this:

'He's dead, he's dead.' Then: 'Gerald, Gerald,' Then more screams. It was Robbie who slapped Clio's face but it was Joss who shouted at her—almost as loudly as her own screams: 'What do you mean, girl? How can he be dead?'

'He's dead,' wailed Clio in a quieter tone. 'I got into the bed, I touched something. It was a scarf. A long woollen scarf! A horrible thing. Red and purple squares.' She gulped. 'I pulled it. It didn't move. I put on the light. It was round his neck. He's dead. Gerald's dead.'

109

'My scarf!' screamed Ellie in her turn. 'That's my scarf!'

What followed was one of the most dreadful New Year's Days that Jemima had ever spent. The Crask headland and its castle was like something under an evil spell. Dawn came late and brought with it lurid red steaks over the North Sea: diabolic colours, thought Jemima.

The police in the person of one solitary officer took a long time to reach them: the nearest police station was after all over twenty-five miles away, and the force in general was occupied by drivers in distress, drunken drivers, and drunks pure and simple. The police doctor, summoned by him, took even longer to arrive; arrangements to take away the corpse—yes, Gerald had been strangled and with Ellie's woollen scarf—would take a while to make. In the meantime the corpse was locked inside the Brown's room, while Robbie, Ellie and of course Clio took refuge in the Big Tower.

No-one could leave the castle; statements would have to be made, evidence taken. The remaining occupants of Crask sat around in the big sitting room, as though in a daze.

At one point Ellie, who seemed personally angry with a situation so clearly devoid of any element of enjoyment, burst out. 'It must have been some tramp. He could have got in by the back door, through that kitchenette. Some maniac. He could still be lurking. And he took my scarf!' Nobody answered her. After a while Robbie patted her hand. But nobody for the time being chose to go and sleep. When Lady Martin was wakened—by Joss—and told of the tragedy, she too joined them: with her curly grey hair, in her tartan dressing-gown, she had the air of some cozy family nanny.

What Lady Martin said to Jemima later that morning was however the reverse of cozy. Joss was talking to the police; Clio was lying down in his room (which he had made over to her); Robbie and Ellie were in the kitchen trying to organise some kind of meal in the absence of any local help at Hogmanay.

'She did it! Of course that wicked Clio Brown did it.' Lady Martin's voice shook slightly in the passion of her conviction; she might have been lobbying a recalcitrant politician for the rights of the forgotten. 'I recognise evil when I see it. People think I'm blind to the bad side of life—but what do they know about me? On the contrary, I've seen so much of it, that I recognise it instantly. Clio Brown has no moral sense. She never had when she flirted with Robbie in the first place, then abandoned him for Gerald, all for the sake of the Brown money. Then she wasn't even grateful to Gerald for that—'

Jemima realised that May Martin, another woman who had married a rich man, was subconsciously contrasting Clio's behaviour with her own: she gathered May had been extremely attentive to Sir Ludwig during their brief and harmonius marriage.

'Now she's done away with him in order to marry Joss and queen it here at Benmuir.' Lady Martin paused in her harangue. 'Yes, Jemima, I'm afraid my nephew Joss is not exactly a moral person either. Clio and Joss: they're alike in that way. Oh ye Gods! Money, and what people will do for it.'

An unbidden thought came to Jemima that Lady Martin could perhaps have prevented all this, whatever it was that had happened, by helping her nephew with

Benmuir. She dismissed the thought. Who was she, Jemima, to say that family feeling should be put before human rights? She herself had no family.

'Listen, my friend,' said Jemima in her most soothing interviewer's manner, patting the tartan clad knee. 'It's out of the question. Clio couldn't have done it. Gerald was alive when she went into the Bottle Dungeon, we know he was, and dead when she came out of it. So she couldn't have done it. No-one gets out of the Bottle Dungeon without help. That motto carved in the stone—how does it go?'

All the time however Jemima was thinking fiercely beneath her tranquil front: I'm right, aren't I? She couldn't have done it, could she? She went over to the Little Tower, we saw her go. Gerald waved her goodbye, we saw him. A few minutes later she was back with us. Then she went down into the dungeon, we watched her, the ladder was pulled up and put aside, we could all see the stone cell from the Big Tower window. She couldn't have got out by herself. There's no way anyone could have got her out without being seen. The boys, above all *Joss:* no, he was here, we were all here. Even when

Joss was dummy, he kept looking over my shoulder. Robbie never left the bridge table. If anyone went to the loo—maybe Ellie did when she was dummy—she would simply have gone to that little turret cloakroom on the same floor; one instant away; you'd have noticed a longer absence.

Jemima pursued her thoughts. And yet Gerald was dead when Clio was released. He must have been. Robbie took her up to her bedroom door and came straight down, we heard him. Clio couldn't have killed him then, there wasn't time. Besides, Gerald's body was beginning to grow cold. Jemima shuddered as she thought: I touched him.

To distract herself, she repeated: 'How does the motto go?'

'Like this. *Initus*—once you're in, *non abeat*—you can't get out. The only Latin I know.' Lady Martin sounded weary. 'Girls in our family weren't taught Latin. Not that it would have been much use to me, as things turned out. I did learn First Aid and nursing, much more useful, handling people the right way.' Her voice trailed away.

Afterwards Jemima would look back on this conversation as crucial, and Lady

Martin as the person who in all fairness was really responsible for solving the case. At the time she merely felt some stirring of comprehension, as though recent events, if looked at from the opposite angle, might be understood altogether differently—and correctly.

Jemima jumped up. 'Will you be all right, May? I need—fresh air.' On her way out of the Big Tower Jemima stopped by the open door to the sitting room. Joss was standing there, looking out of the window. When she reached the ground floor, she could hear Robbie and Ellie in the kitchen. Jemima caught the words: 'My scarf.' Ellie was still complaining. She grabbed her own coat from the pile in the hall, and passed rapidly out of doors. She walked across the grass, towards the stone cell, bending slightly in the wind. Jemima was conscious that Joss must be watching her from the window, as they had watched first Gerald, then Clio, the evening before. The door of the cell was still open; no-one had thought to close it.

Jemima entered. The fetid reek from the open mouth of the Bottle Dungeon seemed to her stronger than ever: a reek of death. After all, if some prisoners had lived, in torment, others had died here. She remembered Clio's provocative comparison of the dungeon to marriage, a state from which she could not emerge without help. Gerald of course, like some of the past prisoners, had emerged from it through death. The stone words were just visible above her head in the dim light. She traced them with her finger.

'*Initus*... Suddenly she understood.

At that moment there was a noise behind her. Jemima turned cautiously round; she did not want to lose her footing. 'Joss! You gave me a fright. I might have hurtled down into the depths.'

'I wouldn't have let that happen. No more tragedies.' Joss was blocking the light so that Jemima could not see his expression.

'How's Clio?'

'As well as can be expected.' It was impossible to tell whether the cliché was intended sarcastically without seeing Joss's face. The effect was to make Jemima eager to get out of the cell, away from the pervasive stink which came from the dungeon into the sea-wind. She moved towards the door but Joss continued to block it.

'Any theories?' he asked. 'Any theories, Jemima Shore Investigator?' He used the title of her television series by which the public generally identified her but he made the words seem threatening. 'Do you buy Ellie's tramp or Ellie's maniac?'

'*Are* there tramps in this remote spot? You tell me. But as for maniacs, I suppose you find them anywhere.'

'Like criminals.'

'Exactly.' Jemima knew her voice was beginning to sound stifled. 'The air, Joss,' she began, 'the air in here—' Then she realised what she must say. 'One thing I do know: nobody in the party could have done it.' May God forgive her for the lie: but like any prisoner she needed to get out.

'Is that so?'

'How could they? We were all together all the time, weren't we? Except for Clio, that is.'

'And she was—here.' Joss stepped forward as though to peer into the hole.

'Quite rare and absolutely horrible.' Jemima was pleased to find her voice was under control. 'No wonder Clio panicked and sounded the bell.'

Joss moved aside. Jemima stepped out.

117

She was now in the full view of the first floor of the Big Tower, where she could make out Robbie and Ellie standing together. They must be able to see her. She was safe. Nevertheless Jemima chose to walk a number of yards away from the stone cell in the direction of the Big Tower. Then she saw Clio coming out of the great door. Her short black hair became rapidly wind blown; she was wearing a parka over the black suit she had worn the night before. Clio came and leant against Joss. He gave the impression of being quite indifferent to what anyone might think of this. Jemima had a fierce impulse to disturb that feline composure. She took a deep breath.

'Yes, you are alike,' she said sharply to Joss. 'Your aunt was right. Not only in your natures but physically alike. Both of you tall with short black hair. How could we tell the difference from the Big Tower? A parka over black trousers. We thought it was Clio. It was you, Joss. After you took May to her room. You killed him, didn't you.' Jemima still addressed Joss. 'You took Ellie's scarf from her room to kill him. Then you made him wave out of the window, took up his arm and manipulated him, handled him. So that we were certain he was alive. Minutes later Clio came back into the sitting room. She'd been downstairs all along. And together you set up the bet. Another piece of handling.'

'What's she saying, darling? Why is she saying these horrible things?' Clio sounded merely plaintive; she still looked perfectly, composedly beautiful.

Joss said nothing. He continued to gaze impassively at Jemima. She was glad to be under the protective gaze of Robbie and Ellie.

'Initus non abeat. Once in, you can't get out. The motto,' cried Jemima. 'But Clio wasn't actually *in* the dungeon when Gerald died. That was all a plot, a distraction to get our attention. She was lurking downstairs among all the coats, finding jerseys there, letting *you* do it, Joss. Afterwards Clio's panic in the dungeon may well have been genuine, ringing that bell that Robbie found. She was alone, she had connived at the murder of her husband: and of course the bell made for another distraction.'

'Prove it,' said Joss coldly to Jemima. To Clio he said: 'Pay no attention, she's mad. Media people! We should never have let

Aunt May bring her. Unhinged!'

'I can't prove it. That's for the police.' As though on cue, Jemima was aware of the distinctive Scottish police car driving towards the gates of the castle to her right. 'All I know is: you were in it together. And you're still in it together: this is one Bottle Dungeon with two prisoners inside it. A desperate kind of marriage: your word, Clio. Until one of you turns on the other, that is.'

As the police car drove nearer, Jemima saw Clio's slanting cat's eyes slide away from Joss. Clio was in deep, as deep as she had been down in those fetid depths. But Clio was going to try to get out. She'll betray him, thought Jemima, and after all he did the killing. What was it May Martin said that afternoon by the dungeon? Some people are survivors.

A Winter Break

Tim Heald

The woman had arrived the night before. The landing had been as tight as it always is on Madeira, though how much that had to do with the configuration of the runway and how much with the machismo of the Portugese pilot she wasn't sure. Her friends had warned her about the landing, so she had not found it as shocking as some of her fellow passengers: gentle, elderly folk with cardigans and plastic macs who clapped with relief as they taxied towards the terminal.

She took a cab to the hotel, checked in and went straight to bed. Even on the package deal the hotel was expensive, but it was essential she stayed there and, thank God, she had squirrelled away a little nest egg of her own. She hardly dared think what she would have done if her mother had not owned a house with spare space in it. The bailiffs had taken everything. She

121

had never spared much sympathy for other people whose companies crashed, always believed, subconsciously, that it served them right and they would bounce back with some new operation in a matter of weeks. She knew better now. Living with her mother and temping was not what she had reckoned on in the days of her pomp as the chairman's wife.

After breakfast on her balcony she wandered down town, strolled along the marina, visited the museum of religious art, explored the market, marvelling at the fruit and grimacing at the long lines of shiny, baleful black espada fish. Espada cropped up on the menu at lunch, fried with boiled potatoes, in an empty restaurant in a street full of empty restaurants where they gave her a glass of sweet and sour sercial wine on the house. Then she looked at some lace and embroidery and bought some interesting leather boots for her son who would be seven years old next week. At tea-time she walked back up the hill past the pink governor's palace, past several shuffling couples she recognised from the aeroplane, past flocks of garish and faintly unsettling bird-of-paradise flowers.

Back at the hotel she kicked off her

shoes and lay on the bed for an hour or so reading a slim volume by J.L Carr, a comforting English novelist of whose work she was particularly fond. At six she started to run a bath, lay in it a long time, then dried slowly and dressed in expensive silk underwear and a tight, short, elegant but simple little black dress. She took care over her make-up and applied just a little too much Chanel No 5 to be quite discreet. For a few moments she stood silently looking at a photograph in a silver frame which she had put on her bedside table as soon as she arrived. Then she leant forward and kissed it lightly, sighed once and went downstairs to the bar.

The man spent the day in his suite.

He spent most of his time in his suite and sometimes didn't leave it for days on end. On December 3rd, the day the woman arrived on her week-long mini-break, he read the previous day's English newspapers and watched his favourite video which was a BBC recording of the 1981 Test series between England and Australia. Once or twice he turned on his short wave radio to listen to the World Service News. Occasionally he would sit at his table and write in pencil on a lined pad. It seemed to cause him difficulty and as often as not he would crumple the page into a ball and throw it in the waste-paper basket. He was trying to write a pseudonymous autobiography.

At one o'clock a maid came with a fillet steak, medium rare, chips and a green salad with a blue cheese dressing. Also a half bottle of quite good claret (Château Talbot). He ate it fast, as if he was used to snatching meals on the hoof between important meetings. After he had finished he belched and spent half an hour looking out of his window at the sea which was grey and rough. Then he went into the bedroom, removed his shoes and lay down on the bed. He lay there for the best part of an hour with his eyes closed but not sleeping. Then he went back to his desk and tried some more writing. When it didn't work he stared out at the sea.

At six he poured himself a large Scotch and ran a bath heavily frothed with Badedas. Afterwards he stood in a towelling bathrobe, smoked a half Corona and looked out at the lights of Funchal. The maid came in to turn the bed down. He eyed her thoughtfully and decided that he would dine in the hotel grill. Because it was a Grand Hotel that meant black tie. He had had a dinner jacket run up by a little man in town and it was fine as far as it went though he regretted the Savile Row number he had owned before.

It was five past seven when he patted his cheeks with Chanel Pour Homme, pocketed his key and walked slowly towards the bar.

The woman sat at a table for two drinking a white wine spritzer and smoking a Marlboro. A pianist in a plum coloured jacket played a superior musical wallpaper medley in which 'A Nightingale Sang in Berkeley Square' was a unifying theme, and barmen and waiters shimmied about with cocktail shakers and saucers of nuts and crisps and translucent cocktail onions. There were several couples and one group of four sitting at other tables. They were late middle-aged to elderly, seemed married, and looked bored. The wives eyed the woman with obvious distaste. She was thirty something, she had shapely legs and just too much make-up. Of course the wives with their pale blue hair and their tinted glasses on gold chains did not like what they saw. The woman saw them looking and knew perfectly well what they were thinking so she stared back at them, crossing her legs and blowing smoke down her nostrils. Then she pretended to study the menu.

When the man came in he enveloped the room with an appraising, all embracing stare, sweeping round the whole area in a smooth arc like the beam of a lighthouse. He was not interested in the couples or the foursome because they were what he had come to expect but as his eyes lit on the woman he paused momentarily. She was looking at him, as was everybody else because it was a quiet night and they were bored and he had made what might be termed 'an entrance'. For a second their eyes locked and then the man continued with his sweep until he reached the barman, smiled glacially and said, 'Good evening, Felipe.'

Felipe inclined his head, reached for a bottle of Chivas Regal on the shelf behind him, poured it over a handful of ice cubes in a heavy tumbler and pushed it across the counter together with the little bowls of things to eat. The man speared two onions with a stick, took a slurp of his drink and seemed to chew on it before swallowing. Then he too fell to studying his menu with an exaggerated display of concentration.

Dinner was a piece of theatre. The woman went through before the man who followed about ten minutes later. She was at a table in a window from which you could see a glitter of stars and city lights. He was seated similarly, but at the far end of the room. Between them lay a no-man's land of empty tables and pockets of monosyllabic couples plus the one quartet. In among them over-dressed waiters and sommeliers shimmered about with bottles of wine in wicker baskets and stacked oversize plates on their arms. Occasionally there would be a whoosh of flame as one of the men ignited alcohol over a slab of beef or a sticky crêpe. The chandeliers and the drapes were theatrical too, although in a half forgotten histrionic style redolent of 1950s Brighton.

The staff and the other guests were half chorus, half audience. On the one hand they contributed to the business of the evening, giving a muffled hubbub and sense of crowd to what would otherwise be an awkward tête-a-tête. On the other hand they were the paying punters, all too aware of the dramatic tension in the air, all agog to see what was going to happen. Every other guest in the dining room was paired off and had been for a minimum of thirty years. Only the one single man and the one lone woman held the potential for excitement and the unexpected. The others knew this and they willed something to happen.

The power of prayer is awesome, even in the dining room of a Grand Hotel in the Atlantic Ocean.

The man bolted his meal and the woman lingered. She was still sipping coffee and toying with her petits fours when he flung down his napkin and pushed back his chair. At the beginning of the meal he had reached his table without passing close to hers, but it would be possible to make the return journey by a different route. If he did he would be so close that it would be positively churlish not to acknowledge her. If he acknowledged her might he not go just a shade further...? After all she was on a week long mini-break and he was old enough, almost, to be her father.

The man smiled at her.

The woman smiled back.

'I wonder,' he said, 'that is to say, would you join me in a liqueur? The hotel has some very fine nineteenth century madeiras. It would be a pleasure to introduce you to one.'

'You're very kind but...'

Perhaps only the English made such a performance of offering and being offered a glass of wine. She accepted, of course, but not before a ritual gavotte of fluttering eyelashes and winsome smiles, of promises implicit yet unstated, of platitudinous pleasantries studded with sub-text of impenetrable complexity. The man and the woman enjoyed a glass of 1893 Madeira together. No more, no less. Not true. Much more, much less. But how and why who knows?

'You're here on holiday?'

It was a wig. Quite a good wig as wigs go, but she could see the straightness of the line between the hair and the scalp, the sudden difference between the straggly real, almost pubic grey stuff at the temples and the straight jet black thatch above the wig-line. And it was ever so slightly crooked. Imperceptible to a casual observer, even perhaps to the *maître d'* in a Grand Hotel, but to her an immediate *faux-pas*.

'Yes. Just a short break.'

'Ah.'

'And you?'

'A longish break.' The man laughed.

The laugh did not come easily. Not just because he seemed not to be a man given to laughter and the laugh therefore seemed devoid of warmth and spontaneity, humour and life, and all that make a laugh worth laughing. It was something physical as well. When he stretched his face the skin somehow moved in the wrong way so that it no longer quite matched the bones beneath. The lines fell wrong and the wrinkles were misplaced. Only a trained observer or someone who knew a great deal about the man would have noticed anything odd.

The woman gave a curious little start when the man laughed, almost as if she had half recognised someone but couldn't remember who they were. The sort of panicky reaction one has when one bumps into someone you know perfectly well but out of context so you can't place them. Like meeting the vicar in a house of ill repute; or a tart in church. Whatever it was the woman checked it instantly and the man seemed not to notice.

It was not a long laugh.

'Have you been here before?'

'No, never.'

'Perhaps I could show you round. The north coast is very fine. Wild with waterfalls. And the drive across the mountains. At Encumeada you can see the north and south coasts. I could arrange a car.'

The woman protested a little but not too much. The man insisted. He said it would be his pleasure. There was nothing, he told her, that could not be put off until tomorrow. Or the day after. Or, come to that, next week or even next year. The truth was that he was bored.

And so, next day, he showed her the west and north of the island. And the day after he took her to the east. He showed her the botanical gardens, the Paul de Serra and the Ribeira da Janela. He pointed out lunar volcanic rock formations and banana plantations and kapok trees. He talked of the history of the island, of Christopher Columbus and of John Blandy who came from Dorset with General Beresford in 1801 and stayed to found a dynasty. He bought her espada fish to eat and vinho verde to drink.

Of himself he said nothing.

He made no sexual advance nor did he make very serious attempts to get to know her better. It was as if he needed only the comfort of company, of having someone around who was not himself. It helped that she was attractive but not, apparently, in a physical sense. He liked to be surrounded by beautiful things but not, necessarily, to touch.

Just once, seeming to notice her wedding ring for the first time, he said, 'You're married?'

'He died,' she said.

'I'm sorry,' he said.

'He killed himself. Money worries. He lost it all.'

'Oh.'

After a little silence she said, 'And you?'

And he said, 'That all seems a very long time ago.'

This was as near to intimacy as they got until the week of the woman's holiday was almost over.

'I wonder,' she said, as they sat at what had now become their usual table, 'if we might go for a walk tomorrow. I would awfully like to stroll along a levada.'

The levadas are the irrigation channels which criss-cross the island. They are a marvel of engineering, passing through mountains and ravines, sometimes in treacherous unlit tunnels. They now double up as a network of beautiful footpaths, affording miraculous views but also what the authors of the best Madeira guidebook describe as 'Danger of vertigo'. The drops can be severe and there are not always railings.

'We could take a picnic,' she said. 'We'll get the driver to drop us off and pick us up again a few hours later.'

He smiled indulgently. Although he was a standard shape and size and could not have been more than fifty-five at worst the man did not look like a walker.

'If that's what you'd like,' he said.

She arranged the alfresco lunch through the kitchens of the hotel. It was not a very Madeiran selection because she wanted it to be a special, simple memorable meal.

Scottish smoked salmon with thinly sliced brown bread, Dublin bay prawns, rare fillet of beef, a hint of truffle, a perfect peach, stilton. To drink, a half bottle of La Grande Dame, another of Latour and to end a glass of hundred year old Blandy's Malmsey. Proper coffee in a thermos. It cost a lot of money and it really did mean that her little nest egg would be well and truly gone. The private detective, of course, had taken the bulk of it but she didn't grudge him. He had done what she wanted.

'Oh, and Joseph,' she said, prettily, 'could you let me have a proper knife? It's murder trying to cut things with a table knife. If you could let me have a real kitchen one. A Sabatier. Otherwise one spends all one's time struggling just to slice bread. And as for meat...' She smiled, as if at a private joke, 'I do want it to go well,' she said, 'It's my only chance to say thank you after all he's done for me.'

Joseph, the chef, nodded and smiled, thinking privately that the man was a lucky fellow.

It was a grand day for a picnic. December in Madeira can be wet and stormy, but the

134

sun was shining as their car hairpinned its way into the mountains, passing from the greenhouse effect of the coastal plain to the eucalyptus and heath trees of the heights. The driver dropped them at Ribeiro Frio and they walked downhill a little until they reached the Levada do Furado tumbling angrily through the woods, gorged with winter rain. The sun dappled the mossy banks and from time to time the path criss-crossed the levada on little stepping stones.

After a while the scenery began to change—the trees became sparser and more windswept, they left behind the last of the red-hot pokers, and the views opened out so that they were able to gaze towards the steep terraces above the north coast villages. Here and there one could pick out a cross gleaming on top of a church spire.

The levada hugged the mountainside and the drop below became ever more precipitous. Presently however they came to a relatively wide ledge of grass where there was more than enough room to spread out and relax. The woman suggested they stop here for lunch and the man seemed happy to acquiesce. She unslung her rucksack and unpacked.

It was warm in the sun and they were sheltered from any wind. It was also very beautiful. To disturb the tranquillity would have been sacrilege, so they said very little. He ate and drank much more than she did though he seemed not to notice that she was only pecking at the food and sipping at the drink.

Finally they arrived at the coffee and the Madeira and he sat, sated and blinking contentedly at the green hillsides and the blue ocean below and beyond.

She was rummaging in the rucksack.

'There's something I want you to see,' she said.

And she passed him her photograph in its silver frame.

He took it, frowning stupidly, like a child being offered an unexpected gift. Then his eyes twitched and he glanced quickly from the picture to her and back.

'Your husband,' he said.

'Yes,' her voice was over-firm now, taut with the effort of seeming super-calm.

'So he...'

'He didn't feel he had any alternative,' she said. 'You took him over, you cleaned him out, you left him with very much less than nothing and then you did your famous bunk. Perhaps he was right. Nothing but creditors, nothing but debts, no future, no prospects, a wife and child to support. So he booked into a cheap hotel with a bottle of Scotch and some sleeping pills, wrote a couple of letters, ran a bath and was found by the chambermaid next morning. Nothing to it really. Happens all the time.'

He stared at her. His face seemed slack and drained, yet it was difficult to read it. Shock, horror...perhaps. Surprise, certainly. Maybe a suggestion of relief, even. Nothing to suggest remorse on the one hand or self-pity on the other.

'How did you find me?'

'Not difficult,' she shrugged. 'I hired a professional. The police didn't seem to find you that interesting. So you'd disappeared with a few million quid but it was mostly small investors, no-one big enough to make an embarrassing fuss. The only person who might have come into that category was probably my husband and he was conveniently out of the way. So why should they use valuable manpower chasing after a vanished swindler when they could be fabricating false evidence against Irish vagrants or beating up black teenagers?

Much easier to write "Missing presumed dead" and forget all about you. I seem to have been practically the only person who wasn't prepared to do the same. My man knew the few plastic surgeons capable of doing the sort of job you needed and it wasn't difficult to find someone to talk. After that one thing led to another.'

He grimaced.

'You'll never be able to prove it. Even if you did you'd never get extradition. I can sit here like Ronnie Biggs, the train robber in Brazil. Stay here as long as I like.'

'Who said anything about proving anything? Or extradition? As far as I'm concerned I'm more than happy that you stay here for the rest of your life.'

He smiled. 'So you want money. Is that what it comes down to?'

'Oh no.' She smiled too. At least she flexed her mouth briefly. There was no humour in the gesture which was more like that of an anaconda about to strike. 'Money itself means nothing to me.'

'What then?'

'I'm going to kill you.'

A sudden deft gesture and the hotel kitchen knife, six inches of well honed stainless steel, lay glistening in her right hand.

'I'm rather good with a knife,' she said, 'I found a friendly ex-SAS bloke who gave me a few lessons. I have to say he was quite impressed. Unlike you, I am extremely fit and I can give you at least twenty years. So whatever you do, you haven't a chance.'

He said nothing, just looked at her quietly and moistened his lips.

'Do you have anything to say?'

He shook his head, still staring at her, unblinking.

'Then stand up.'

He stood. There were breadcrumbs on the front of his jacket and a drop of claret on his shirt.

She stood, too, and took a pace towards him, knife raised now, so that it's point was aimed at his jugular six feet away.

Instinctively he backed off. He did not seem particularly frightened, however. Almost resigned. His face—that alien plastic mask—gave nothing away. But he still reversed, realising perhaps that a struggle would indeed be useless as well, perhaps, as undignified. In a curious way he seemed to accept the situation, wanting only to carry it off with the correct style which perhaps was why he brushed at the crumbs. He wanted to die with a clean front.

She took another step towards him. He took one back. She made a feint and he tottered two half steps away. She lunged—or pretended to and as he, frightened now despite himself, recoiled from the stroke, his back foot went over the edge of the precipice and came down on thin air. He staggered. She lunged again. He fell back. His mouth opened and his arms leaped high to grab on to something, anything, to steady himself but there was nothing there. Again she lunged, knife steady in her fist, eyes fixed on his throat, but there was no need.

He only screamed after he went over the cliff. The sound echoed around the mountains for what seemed like an eternity, hanging in the air, bouncing like the man's body from one volcanic outcrop to another until at last it faded away into a total silence.

She had not even touched him. It was the sort of accident that could have happened to almost anyone.

The knife fell from her hand and, silently, the woman began to sob.

Strangers on a Bus

Reginald Hill

He was two hundred yards from the stop when the bus overtook him.

There were three people waiting. It was pay-as-you-enter. Fifteen seconds apiece. Forty-five seconds to do two hundred yards. Him, George Donjon, St Eric's Junior School fifty-yard champion twice in the nineteen-sixties. A doddle.

He started to run.

A specialist should stick to his speciality.

He was fine for the fifty. Then things fell apart. His knees started to crumble, his lungs to puncture, his eyeballs to pop. By the time he collapsed against the closed door, his heaving heart was trying to exit through his gaping mouth.

The driver examined the purple face flattened against the misting window, shook his head, and pressed the button that re-opened the door.

'You want to try getting up in the

morning, mate,' he said.

'Thanks—a—sodding—million,' gasped George.

He collapsed in the first vacant seat, slumping heavily against a man in an outmoded safari suit.

'You OK?' said the stranger anxiously.

'You blind? Do I look OK?'

It took three stops for George to re-establish something like normal service to his nerve centres. With muscular control came a sense of his ungraciousness and he said to his neighbour, 'I'm sorry, I didn't mean to be rude. It's the car. Bloody thing wouldn't start.'

'Snap,' said the man.

'Sorry?'

'Same thing. Car let me down so I had to run for the bus.'

'You're obviously fitter than me.'

'You should've seen me when I got on. I made you look like Carl Lewis.'

They got off at the same stop, but went different ways. George hurried along the pavement at a speed which had him gasping again, but he was still ten minutes late.

Ferguson, the manager, was going through his desk.

'Need the Maxco figures,' he said shortly. 'I rang down but you weren't here.'

'Sorry. It's the car, bloody thing wouldn't start again.'

'Get a new one,' growled Ferguson who managed to roll 'r's even when there weren't any.

'I bloody would if you gave me a decent wage, you Scotch git,' snarled George. But not until he was alone. And even then, under his breath.

He got his revenge by leaving early, but only because Ferguson had gone north to a conference. The receptionist, a pretty redhead with an available smile, raised her eyebrows quizzically.

George responded with what he thought of as his rake-hell grin and said, 'Mustn't be late twice in one day!' as he swept past her.

When he got home he saw a familiar behind sticking out from under the bonnet of his car. Madge, his wife, was standing on the house steps, and she cried preemptively, 'George, isn't it nice, I was telling Sandra about the car, and Barry came round to see if there was anything he could do.'

As she pecked his cheek, she hissed, 'Be polite.'

'Aren't I always?' muttered George. It wasn't strictly true. Barry Briggs had many excellent qualities. He was kind, considerate, and helpful. He was also married to Madge's very best friend, Sandra. But even such pluses couldn't always compensate for the fact that he was a know-it-all bore.

The main thing about which he knew-it-all was traffic. He was a police inspector in charge of the traffic branch of the local force and he brought to his work a passionate commitment that most men save for religion or association football. A spin-off from this was an intuitive understanding of the inner workings of a car. George tended to be sceptical, if not downright cynical, about this claimed expertise. On the other hand, he'd never yet met a mechanic he'd have trusted to screw the top on a sauce bottle, and at least Barry came free. So he approached him now with a bright bonhomie.

'Hi, Barry, how's it looking?'

'Hello there, George. I think I've got to the bottom of it. Tappets, that's the giveaway. You really should listen, George.

Man who ignores what his tappets are telling him is heading for trouble, know what I mean?'

George winced. Barry had various verbal tics, all of which were irritating, and this one most of all.

'Yes, I think I know what you mean, Barry,' he said seriously. 'Man who ignores his tappets is heading for trouble, is that it?'

'Got it in one, George,' said Barry. 'Nearly done. Tell Madge she can start brewing up. Nothing like the cup that cheers to round off a bit of hard graft, know what I mean?'

It would be cheaper to ring the garage, thought George gloomily.

But a few minutes later as he listened to his engine running sweetly and smoothly, he had to admit that Barry seemed to have done the trick.

Nevertheless he rose bright and early the next morning and approached the vehicle with considerable distrust. It behaved perfectly, and he had the satisfaction of being well established at his desk when Ferguson stuck his head through the door on his way upstairs.

'I knew the bastard would check up on

me,' he told Madge that night. 'It's all right for him. If the company bought *me* a new Granada very year, I'd get there on time every day too.'

'Ours isn't an old car,' said Madge defensively.

'No. It just thinks it is. Premature automotive Alzheimer's, that's what it's got. From time to time it just forgets how to start.'

Two days later it forgot again. This time he didn't hang around trying to fix it. Pausing only to curse Barry Briggs and tell Madge to ring the garage, he set off with plenty of time to spare.

The bus passed him when he was still a hundred yards from the stop.

'You're early,' he gasped as he pulled himself aboard.

'There's no pleasing some people,' said the driver.

George found an unoccupied double seat. As the bus set off, someone tapped him on the shoulder. It was the man in the safari suit.

'Trouble again?' he said.

'You could say that. And you?'

'Need you ask? It spent a day under the care of my local mechanical genius. Cured,

146

he said. I turned the key. Nothing! Bloody marvellous, eh?'

George laughed sympathetically, and the man was encouraged to move forward alongside him.

'Tony Lorton,' he said, offering his hand.

'George Donjon. So what did your genius say?'

'Blamed the car, of course. Mind you, he's got a point. It's been a bummer since the day I got it. This is the third garage I've tried, so they can't all be incompetent, can they? I wish I'd never seen the sodding thing.'

'I know the feeling,' said George. 'I've thought of leaving mine all night with the window open and the key in the ignition hoping some joy-rider would nick it and set it alight when he's done. Trouble is, it probably wouldn't start!'

He was late for work again. Ferguson was Celtically sarcastic. George would dearly have loved to tell him to stuff it, but his surreptitious forays into the job market had taught him that in the current economic clime, no-one was buying what he had to sell.

Despising himself, he made sure his

departure that evening coincided with Ferguson's. All he got in reply to his cheerful goodnight was a Gaelic grunt and the door in his face.

Cupping his ear in his hand, George said, 'Did you catch that?' to the receptionist who was putting on her coat.

'Sorry, I don't speak Scotch,' she said smiling.

'Bet you drink it though,' said George. 'Care to join me?'

He got home an hour late.

'Bloody buses,' he said to Madge. 'Did the garage come?'

'Yes. They tinkered for half an hour. Said it should be all right now.'

'Hah!'

But it started, and continued to start first time for over a week.

Then, on the morning of the monthly sales conference, it had a relapse. Lulled by its previous good behaviour, he wasted precious time trying to coax a response and ended up having to do a three hundred yard dash to get on the bus. It was packed this morning and he had to stand. Tony Lorton was sitting near the back. He caught George's eye and mouthed, 'Trouble?' Grimly George nodded and got the sad sympathetic smile of a fellow sufferer.

He was late for the conference, let himself be irritated into bandying words with Ferguson, had a thoroughly unpleasant day, and when he said, 'Fancy a drink?' to the receptionist, she replied primly. 'Sorry, Mr Donjon, I'm washing my hair tonight.'

Bitch! he thought. She knows something. Or guesses. Please, God, don't let them make me redundant. It's that bloody car. Bloody, bloody car!

He really needed a drink, with or without company, and he turned into the Blue Boar opposite the bus-stop.

'Vodka,' he said. 'Big one.'

'Let me get that.'

It was Tony Lorton with a pint mug in his hand.

'It's a double,' warned George.

'That's OK. You look like a man who needs a double. Let's sit over here. We can see the bus coming from the window.'

They sat and talked with the freedom of two men with a common grievance.

'It's Catch Twenty-two,' said George. 'If I had its book value as cash in hand, I could wave it under a dealer's nose, and with the present state of the trade, get something really decent. But as a trade-in, it's practically worthless. They don't want to know. As for selling it privately...'

'I tried that,' said Tony. 'Took it for a test drive. Cost me twenty quid for a tow, plus this punter made me cough up for a taxi.'

'And you paid?'

'He was built like Arnold Schwarzenegger. Another?'

'My shout,' said George.

When he came back from the bar, he said, 'Wasn't that the bus?'

'Probably. Never mind, eh? Like women, there's always another one coming along.'

They laughed like good old boys and after another round were as relaxed as old friends.

'It's even worse for me, George,' said Tony with tipsy seriousness. 'I'm living out on the Langland Rise development, you know it? Right on the edge, next to the playing fields. It's a mile and a half to the nearest bus stop. Without my car, I'm knackered. But with it I'm knackered, too! I mean, all it does is cost me money that I can't afford. And have you noticed how they always break down at the most awkward and usually most expensive times? If I could only cut my losses and get rid of it... But like you say, there's no way. Unless...'

He regarded George speculatively over the rim of his glass.

'Unless what?' said George.

'The other day in the bus you said something about the best thing that could happen would be for someone to steal your car and write it off. Then you'd get the full book value, cash in hand.'

'That's right. Dream scenario. Fancy the job, do you, Tony? Worth a couple of drinks!'

'More than that, I'd say, George,' said Tony softly. 'One good turn would deserve another, that's how I see it.'

George sipped his drink. He felt very sharply focused, very much in control.

'You're not serious?' he said.

'I don't know,' said Tony. 'But think about it. Like you said, it happens all the time. Tearaways joy-riding, then torching the car for kicks. Why do you think our premiums are so high?'

'Sure, but it probably also happens all the time that guys like you and me decide they'd rather have the money than the car and try a do-it-yourself job. They're not daft, insurance claim investigators.'

'Of course they're not,' said Tony, glancing round the bar and pulling his chair closer to the table. 'But that's the beauty of this scheme of ours. You fix yourself up with a nice little alibi for the night the car goes missing. What you need is a good reliable witness, someone rock solid...'

'No problem,' said George determined not to be outdone in criminal insouciance. 'I've got a sure fire winner. Name of Briggs. Wait till you hear this. Police Inspector Barry Briggs!'

'You're kidding? A cop? That's perfect,' said Tony, much impressed. 'What's he like though? You don't want someone who's got a naturally suspicious mind.'

'No, he's not that kind of cop. More your dull old plod. He's king of traffic down the local nick, and that's all he's interested in. His wife and mine are mates. Now she's a luscious little thing, God knows how she puts up with old Barry. Hey, you know what she told me once? She said he's got a prick like a traffic light. It lights up in strict sequence, and you get a ticket if you try to jump it!'

He felt a small pang of guilt at thus drunkenly betraying Sandra's confidence, but it seemed worth it when Tony laughed so much, he almost choked on his beer.

'And he'd give you an alibi?' he said frothily.

'No problem. It's all set up. First Saturday of every month the four of us go to the dinner dance at Crichton Manor. And here's the best of it, Barry doesn't drink, so he always does the driving.'

'Perfect! With me it's every Tuesday. It's as good an alibi as yours, only you mustn't laugh. My wife and I do a bit of singing. Every Tuesday we go to choir practice.'

'Choir practice!' hooted George.

'That's right. Local church hall. It's about half a mile and we always walk it. And you know who runs the choir? The vicar! A clergyman and a cop. No beating that for witnesses!'

'No,' agreed George. 'So what precisely happens?'

'OK, let's get down to cases. You get home from the dance. The car's gone! Alarm, despondency! Inform the police. That's easy, you'll be with the police. Next day it's found on the Common. A burnt-out shell. You're completely in the clear. And even if they did cast a suspicious eye over your friends and acquaintances, what's to find? Nothing. That's the real beauty of it. As far as you and me are concerned, there's no connection whatsoever.'

'We're having a drink together,' objected George.

'So what? No-one's taking our pictures. We're just a couple of guys who sometimes travel on the same bus. Where's the link? OK, if it'll make you feel better, from now on, if we meet, we don't know each other. In any case, once we've got our insurance money, we'll be buying cars that work, so there'll be no reason for either of us to use the bus again.'

It had an elegant logic which pleased George greatly. Spurred to show he too was a man of practicalities, he said, 'But how do we get into the cars? And we'd need to hot-wire them, isn't that the term? How do we do that?'

'You've got a spare key, haven't you?' said Tony. 'Tape it under the rear bumper. I keep one there already, for emergencies.'

'But won't the police know there hasn't been a break-in?'

'When the car's a burnt-out shell? Do

me a favour! So, are you in or out?'

'Of course I'm bloody in,' cried George, putting on his rake-hell look. 'Let's have a drink on it.'

They had another drink, then exchanged addresses and car details. When the next bus came into view, George rose. Tony didn't move.

'Not coming?' asked George.

'Not yet. Anyway let's start as we mean to go on. From now on we're strangers, right.'

'Right,' said George. 'Well, goodnight, stranger!'

This struck him as the height of wit and he went out into the night, chuckling. His good humour stayed with him all the way home and even survived the discovery that this was one of Madge's evening class nights and she'd left him a frosty note on the table and a frazzled dinner in the oven.

It wasn't till he woke the next morning with a splitting headache that he gave what had passed in the pub any real consideration.

It was, he soon decided, just an unusual example of the pub fantasy, a pleasant change from the more common areas of erotic reminiscence, plans to walk the Pennine Way, and proposals to tell the boss exactly what you thought of him the following morning.

He put it out of his mind and it made no effort to re-enter till the night of the next Crichton Manor dinner dance. During this time the car had behaved impeccably. Now as he looked at it parked outside his terraced house, an uneasy memory of the night in the Blue Boar flitted through his mind. It was quickly flapped away. Drunken fantasy! And besides, the spare key was firmly locked in his bureau drawer.

'Come on, George,' said Barry through the window of his Cavalier. 'Or I'll have to arrest you for loitering, know what I mean?'

He found that Madge, who had occasional eruptions of female assertiveness, had taken his usual place alongside Barry in the front.

'No need for us always to look like a Coronation Street excursion,' she said in response to his raised eyebrows.

If she thought she was putting him down, she was wrong. He had no objection whatsoever to squeezing into the shadowy rear seat alongside Sandra. One hot day last summer he'd called at Barry's house to return some tools he'd borrowed. Barry had been on duty and Sandra was sunbathing on the patio in a bikini which provided less cover than small-print insurance. One thing had led to another, and the other to the bedroom. They'd enjoyed themselves so much, it seemed silly not to repeat the exercise. After a couple of months George had wondered if things were getting serious, and if so, how did he feel about it? But when he dropped a hint of this to Sandra, she had rolled away from him, shaking with laughter.

'What's up?' he said.

'George, you're great fun to fuck with, but don't imagine for one moment I've any intention of getting into a relationship with you!'

He'd looked so hurt that she had felt constrained to soothe him with sexual flattery. This was when she'd produced the traffic light simile, her first and only criticism of her husband. And when George had tried to reply in kind with a little light satire on Madge's growing indifference to sexual activity, she'd cut him off coolly, saying, 'That's enough, George. You're just the guy I screw with, but Madge is my best friend.'

The affair had petered out after that, but with no acrimony, and when they pressed close on the dance floor, the memory of what had been between them went a long way to compensating for Barry's conversation. Sitting thigh to thigh in the back of the car got the evening off to a grand start, and when he and Sandra danced a slow waltz together, he felt as if their bodies were melting into each other's.

When they got back to the table they found that Barry had redistributed the cutlery and condiments to demonstrate how three key point accidents could bring the whole district to a standstill.

'At the end of the day, gridlock's a real statistical inevitability, know what I mean, George?' he said.

George examined the table critically, then said, 'This looks like a job for Supermouth!' And, seizing the bread roll which marked the gridlock's epicentre, he began to eat it.

Even Barry laughed, and this good mood spread out to cover the whole of the evening so that for once it was with genuine pleasure that George said, 'That was great, Barry. I really enjoyed it,' as they were dropped off outside their house.

Then Madge said, 'George, where's the car?'

And the alcoholic vapours burned off his mind like brandy off a Christmas pudding.

'It's gone,' he said abruptly. 'Oh shit.'

Something in his intonation made the others look at him for a moment, but soon they were too busy in their own roles—Madge the bereaved wife, Sandra the sympathetic friend, Barry the man in charge—to pay any special attention to him.

It could of course be a professional job, thought George. More likely, just an opportunist joy-rider. What was most unlikely was that it had anything to do with Tony Lorton. For God's sake, how could he get into the car and start the engine without a key? No, it had to be one of those coincidences that probably happen so often they're not even worth talking about.

With this certainty, he was able to fall into his role of angry victim with some panache.

Barry was for once talking reassuring sense.

'If it's a pro job, that's it. Change the plates and it'll be on someone's forecourt tomorrow. That make, that colour, no need for a paint job, know what I mean? You can kiss it goodbye. Not that that would bother you too much, eh, George? All the grief that car gave you, I daresay you won't be sorry to see the back of it.'

He smiled as he spoke, but for a moment George found himself looking at Barry as a real cop rather than an overblown traffic warden.

It would have been easy to over-react to the comment. Instead, he said seriously, 'What about joy-riders, Barry?'

'Possible. If it is one of those lunatics, you'd better hope he totals it. An hour of hotdrags and handbrake turns can put ten years on a car, but try telling your insurers that the clutch, suspension and gears were all right before, know what I mean? Ah, here they come, we'll soon get things moving.'

The first police car came belling down the street. With Barry's help the official side of reporting the theft was carried out very swiftly, and it wasn't too long

160

after their normal time that the Donjons climbed into bed.

To his surprise George found himself ready to slip off into sleep almost immediately. Then Madge's voice came drifting out of the dark.

'I don't want anyone hurt, but it would be rather nice if whoever took the car wrecked it and we got the money, wouldn't it, George?'

'I wouldn't object,' said George. 'And I can't say I'd be much bothered if the sod who took it totalled himself at the same time.'

This idea had an interesting side effect on both of them. Madge's hand slipped down his belly as if to a gear lever.

'Vroom, vroom,' she said.

After that sleep was postponed for a while.

He was woken early next morning by the phone. It was Barry.

'Thought you'd like to know, they've found it. Looks like joy-riders. It's a write-off, I'm afraid. Someone dropped a match in the tank. Still, no cloud without a silver lining, know what I mean? The insurers will have to cough up full whack.'

'All the same,' said George, thinking a

token protest was in order. 'Where was it, by the way?'

'Somewhere up on the Common,' said Barry.

The Common. Just as Tony had suggested. But so what? It was the obvious place to dump a car. That was why Tony had suggested it. He conjured up a mental picture of the man. Narrow face, a weak mouth, rather watery eyes, thinning wispy blond hair. And that awful safari suit hanging on his skinny body!

It was the picture of a loser, someone who wouldn't dare to even dream big without the help of alcohol. Not someone with the skills and nerve necessary to pull a trick like this.

No, there was no need to worry about Tony Lorton. And it certainly wasn't in order to avoid meeting him that during the carless days that followed, he started catching an earlier bus. It just seemed a wise precaution with things the way they were at work to make sure he wasn't late.

And it really paid off. News of his loss touched a law-and-order nerve in Ferguson whose vicarious indignation, plus George's new punctuality, mellowed his attitude to a patronising jocularity. The redhaired receptionist had started smiling again, and the insurance company assured him that once the paperwork was out of the way, he'd be receiving a cheque for the full market value.

Then he got onto the bus one morning and there was Tony, sitting in the front row.

Their eyes met. A little smile tugged at Tony's mouth and his left eyelash fluttered in a quick wink.

He didn't look at all like a loser. In fact, far from being weedy, his muscular body strained at his safari suit, and his thin face was knowing and streetwise, not weak.

George went to the back of the bus, his heart pounding.

But it still meant nothing; it *had* to mean nothing.

The insurers rang up that morning to say the cheque was in the post.

He'd already spent some time checking out the car dealers. As forecast, the prospect of cash in hand had won him a prodigal's welcome, and he'd negotiated a substantial discount on a low mileage Japanese model with a top rating for reliability. Barry Briggs had checked it out and confirmed his choice, Madge approved the colour, and Sandra who came along for a full test drive remarked in a vibrant, sultry voice which might have had a man less complacent than Barry taking notice, how *exceedingly* comfortable the back seat was.

The cheque arrived, the deal was struck, and with great relief on several fronts George said goodbye to the bus.

For the next few weeks everything was perfect. The car started first time every morning; his new relationship with Ferguson blossomed to the point where they started having the occasional drink together after work; and this excuse for being home late, which Madge, who was very ambitious for him, actually encouraged, provided the perfect cover for drinks with the redhaired receptionist, and ultimately more than drinks in the back of his new car in the empty office car park.

Then one dusky evening as he relaxed, sated, in the exceedingly comfortable rear seat, waiting for the receptionist's two-seater to pull out of the car park, a figure detached itself from the entrance and came swiftly towards him.

It was Tony. He pulled open the door and climbed in.

'Enjoy that, did you?'

'What do you mean?'

'Come on, George. Nice squashy suspension, these things. You got a real sway on.'

'Now look here...'

'No, *you* look. What the hell's going on? It's nearly two months now. That's eight Tuesdays. It's playing hell with my descant.'

George took a deep breath. He was on the whole a man who would take a long diversion to avoid a confrontation, but when a head-on collision was inevitable, he reckoned to fight his corner as well as anyone.

'You're saying it was you who stole my car, right?' he said.

'Naturally. As per our agreement,' said Tony.

'Frankly, I don't believe you,' said George. 'And even if you did, so what? There *was* no agreement, just a couple of guys fantasising in a pub.'

He kept his tone light and friendly, leaving the way open for an easy retreat, and for a few moments it seemed as if Tony might be going to retire gracefully.

'I can see how you might feel that way,

George,' he said with matching amiability. 'In your shoes, insurance company happy, new car in the drive, I might react much the same. I mean, if you can get what you want without the hassle of paying for it, only a mug coughs up. Specially if there's nothing the other guy can do except go to the police and incriminate himself. Right?'

'That's how it looks to me,' agreed George. 'But like I say, I reckon you're just chancing your arm. It was a coincidence my car got wrecked. I know for a fact you had nothing to do with it.'

'Because you didn't leave the key taped to the bumper like we arranged?' said Tony smiling. 'Fair deduction, I suppose. Except, how do I know you didn't leave the key? But it makes no odds, George. You're sticking to your side of the bargain, because if you don't...'

George tensed his muscles. The point about the key was well made, but it made no difference. If necessary, he'd let himself be driven to physical violence to get rid of Tony, but nothing was going to turn him into a car thief and arsonist.

'If I don't what?' he said.

'If you don't, I'll post your wife and

your boss copies of these.'

Tony dropped some photos into his lap. They'd been taken with a zoom lens. Individually they didn't show all that much: the receptionist going towards George's car; George looking round rather furtively as he ushered her into the back seat; the pair of them (it could have been anyone) embracing; a bare white leg (it could have been anyone's) kicking in the air over the front seat head restraint: but in sequence... He flinched as he contemplated Madge's Puritanical and Ferguson's Presbyterian reaction.

Tony was getting out of the car. He stretched his arms and flexed his muscles.

'They don't give you much room in these things, do they? I really don't know how you manage, George, and being so creative. So, that's settled. Next Tuesday. Me and the wife go out at seven thirty, back any time after ten. I'll leave the car parked in the drive alongside the house. There's just the playing field on that side, so you won't be overlooked. And George, if the car won't start, don't just walk away, or I'll be taking a little walk down to the post box. Torch the bloody thing where it stands!'

He strolled away, Robert Mitchum in an old movie, slow and easy.

It was Wednesday night, which gave George six days to wrestle with his conscience.

It took only one of them to acknowledge it wasn't his conscience he was wrestling with but fear.

Which terrified him more—car theft and arson, or the prospect of losing both his job and his marriage?

Put like that there was no competition, except that one required action, the other inaction. Reduced to essentials, the question was, did he have the bottle?

Masculine pride said yes. After all, strictly speaking it wasn't theft. In the final analysis, he'd be driving the car away with the owner's permission, wouldn't he? Which left the arson. Even that was at the owner's instigation, so where was the crime? Conspiracy to defraud a car insurance company? Any decent legal system would give you medals for that!

And so he screwed his courage to the sticking place. And felt it oozing out of every orifice as he approached the Langland Rise Estate the following Tuesday night.

The one good, or bad, thing was that

it was easy for him to get out of the house on Tuesdays. Madge went to evening classes twice a week with Sandra. Musical Appreciation: Bach to Bruckner on Tuesdays, and Catalan cooking on Thursdays. Or perhaps it was the other way round. Whatever, it meant he didn't have to find an excuse for downing several large whiskies before leaving the house dressed like Bill Sikes.

Logistics, as well as the drink, required that he made the approach on foot. He estimated half an hour to Tony's house. He'd picked a spot on the Common from which he could get back home in forty-five minutes. Plus whatever it took him for the job itself, he shouldn't be out of the house for much over a couple of hours, and as Madge and Sandra always went for a drink after their class, he had plenty of time in hand. Piece of cake!

But the walk in the fresh night air had soon burnt the Dutch courage out of him, and as he walked along the deserted pavements of the Langland Rise Estate, he felt that behind every curtain, curious eyes were marking his progress. Certainly if anyone *was* watching, they could have little doubt about where he was going once he'd turned into the cul-de-sac where Lorton lived. There were only three houses here, all on the same side, facing a coppice of birch, with Tony's the last one, separated from the dark emptiness of the playing field by a five-foot chain link fence.

But hesitation would only rouse suspicion. He turned confidently into the drive and thankfully plunged into the shadows at the far side of the house.

Here at least he was free from prying eyes. The car was there, as promised. He ran his hand under the bumper. The key was there too, in a magnetic box with a circlet of putty and covered in tape. Tony was taking no chances.

He opened the driver's door and got in. Now was the crucial moment. An engine starting, a car driving away from an empty house...he could only pray there was something good and noisy on television.

He said the prayer and turned the key.

Nothing.

He tried again.

Still nothing. Quite dead. Flat as a pancake.

He began to laugh. The joke had come true. How can you steal a car that won't start?

But the laughter didn't last long. Tony had foreseen this possibility—or excuse. *Torch the bloody thing where it stands!*

He got out and examined the situation. It was perfectly feasible. On this side of the house there was a blank wall except for a small frosted window, presumably a cloakroom, near the front corner, and a kitchen door near the back.

The car was parked midway between these two features and well away from the wall itself. A bonfire here was unlikely to do more than scorch a bit of paintwork. And even if it did, what the hell? This was Tony Lorton's house, Tony Lorton's idea!

He unlocked the petrol cap. From his pocket he took a roll of thick bandage which he fed into the tank. He was rather proud of this foresight. Lobbing a lighted match into the tank sounded simple, but he didn't fancy being that close when the thing went up. Once he'd got the whole length of the bandage soaked, he trailed it out of the filler hole. His first idea was to light it and then run like hell down the street, but there could be people about at this time of night, and when they heard the bang, they'd take notice of a running man. The clever move would be to make his escape across the playing field. Another bit of foresight had put a torch in his pocket, so there'd be no trouble about seeing his way. Getting over the chain link fence was the only problem but he managed this with the aid of a dustbin he found round the back of the house. Then he pulled the petrol soaked bandage through the fence, took a deep breath, and struck a match.

It would have been wise to take off immediately, but no man who had ever lit a firework on November the Fifth could have turned away without watching the effect.

The fuse itself was rather disappointing, a small blue flame dancing along in a sedate saraband till it climbed laboriously up the side of the car and vanished into the tank.

Then it was bonfire night. The tank went up with a whoomph that made him congratulate himself on keeping his distance. Flames engulfed the car from boot to bonnet just like they did in the movies.

But it didn't end there...Incredibly, horrifyingly, flames ran out of the car too, snaking across the drive, no saraband this but a leaping tarantella which hit the door and the window in a frenzy of fire and imploded into the house.

He stood there, unable to believe what was happening.

There were shouts, sirens, lights waving, footsteps running, figures scaling the fence into the playing field. And still he didn't move, not till a pair of uniformed policemen cuffed his hands behind his back and more or less hurled him over the fence into the arms of another two who frogmarched him into the street.

There were at least six police cars there. He was thrust roughly into one of them, banging his head on the door sill. The blow made him dizzy, but hardly dizzier than the devastating sequence of events which he now discovered had not reached their climax.

That came when the front door of the house opened like a pantomime trap to let out a great puff of smoke in the midst of which he glimpsed a group of people. Some of them were policemen, but they were supporting two figures, doubled up and retching, who were clearly not official. They were a man and a woman. They were both stark naked. And when they straightened up in the fresh night air, he

173

recognised, though he could not believe he recognised, the woman.

It was Madge.

They charged him with attempted murder.

He told his story to the CID men who interrogated him, and they laughed and said, 'That'll get you an extra five years, mate.'

He told it to his solicitor whose patience gave out at the third time of hearing.

'Believe me, Mr Donjon,' he said. 'I've got nothing against my clients lying. The system almost demands that most defendants tell lies. But the whole point of lying is to sound believable. Unless of course you are hoping to enter a plea of insanity?'

Finally Barry Briggs came to see him.

'Didn't come sooner, George. Conflict of loyalties, know what I mean?'

'It's good of you to come now,' said George wretchedly. 'Barry, I'm in deep crap, I don't understand any of this. Madge and that man...'

'Tony Lorton? Bastard. The merry widower they call him on the estate. I'm sorry Sandra got mixed up in the cover-up. Night classes! I've never cared for them myself. I've had words with her about it, believe me. Call yourself a friend, I said. What did you think you were playing at, letting Madge get mixed up with a man like Lorton...'

'No, Barry!' cried George desperately. 'That man I saw wasn't Lorton, the one with Madge, I mean. Tony Lorton was the man I met on the bus...'

'George, stay cool,' interrupted Barry gently. 'That's why I knew I had to come, a friend in need, know what I mean? I heard about this daft story you're trying to get away with. Believe it or not, our CID lot have got hearts. Talk to your mate, they said to me. Tell him to get his act together. Mental breakdown's fine, pressure of work, trick-cyclist on the stand, soapy judge and soft jury, it might work. But this way's just stupid!'

'But it's true,' insisted George passionately. 'It's true.'

Barry Briggs shook his head sadly.

'OK, George,' he said like a kind uncle talking to a recalcitrant child. 'I believe you. At least, I believe you believe yourself. But it changes nothing. It's what the court believes that matters. Sometimes you've got to box clever, play the system, go with the flow, know what I mean?'

'Know what you mean? Know what you mean?' yelled George, all his frustration and bewilderment finally erupting. 'How the hell can I know what you mean when all you ever do is pour out meaningless garbage and tired old clichés? I sometimes wonder if you know what you mean yourself, Barry.'

Even before the outburst was over he was ashamed of it. Something was happening to him, he didn't know what, and he needed to lash out. But of all the people within lashing reach, Barry Briggs was surely the one who least deserved it.

The inspector had risen, his face expressionless.

'Barry, I'm sorry. That was unforgiveable of me. It's just all of this pressure...I'm sorry...'

'That's all right, old boy,' said Barry. 'I understand. You're under great strain. Different people deal with that in different ways, horses for courses, know what I mean? But don't forget what I told you. My advice is, throw yourself on the mercy of the court. These judges are human too, and believe me, they've seen it all. What they don't know about human nature

176

isn't worth knowing. They'll understand what a shock it must be to the system when a man finds out his wife's screwing somebody else. And they'll appreciate the extraordinary antics such a shock can drive a man to. Any man. Even a judge. Even, believe it or not, a dull old plod with a prick like a traffic light. Know what I mean, George? Know what I mean?'

And George sat staring at the cell door long after it had closed behind his friend, not knowing if he knew what he meant or not.

Long Shot

Graham Ison

From his room over the army recruiting office in Great Scotland Yard, David Pinder could hear the crowds cheering in Whitehall and shouting for Churchill. Pinder had been only one year old on Armistice Day in 1918 and obviously could remember nothing about it even though he had been there with his parents—Pinder's father had been a captain, too, on leave from France—and they had often told him, in later years, that the people had gone wild, milling along that same Whitehall, through Admiralty Arch and down The Mall, singing, cheering, dancing and kissing, and demanding that the King and Queen appear on the balcony of Buckingham Palace.

Although today's celebrations marked only the end of the war in Europe and British soldiers were still being killed by the Japanese in the Far East, crowds were here again, singing and cheering, filling once more the vast arena in front of the Palace and calling, over and over again, for the present King and Queen.

'Sir!'

Pinder turned from the window at the sharp double tap of boots on the linoleum-covered floor.

The military police corporal cut his arm away from the salute and remained at attention. 'There's a man outside who wants to see you, sir.'

'A soldier?'

'Says he's been discharged, sir. Gives the name of Weston.'

'What does he want?'

'Says he wishes to report a crime, sir.'

Pinder smiled. 'What does he think this is, a police station?'

The corporal's mouth twitched slightly. 'Says it's a military crime, sir.'

'What is he? Sand-happy?'

'Difficult to tell, sir.' Both the corporal and Captain Pinder wore the riband of the Africa Star and each had spent some time in the Middle East trying to distinguish between deliberate desertion and the mental stress brought about by honest fear and long periods in the desert.

180

'Better show him in then,' said Pinder. 'Got nothing else to do.' He tugged at the waistband of his battledress tunic.

The corporal held open the door. 'This is Captain Pinder, Mr Weston,' he said.

Although he was in plain clothes, the man who was shown into Pinder's office was every inch a soldier. He held himself briefly to attention and waited.

'Good afternoon.' Pinder made to shake hands.

Weston paused and then held out his left hand. 'Most of my other arm's in Normandy somewhere, sir,' he said and Pinder noticed the black-gloved hand that hung stiffly from Weston's right sleeve.

'Sit down, Mr Weston. I understand that you've been demobbed.'

'Yes, sir. Invalided out last Christmas ...after eighteen years service.' Weston sounded bitter. 'Sergeant, Middlesex Rifles, sir.' He sat in the wooden armchair in front of Pinder's desk. 'Not much of a pension, neither.'

Pinder nodded sympathetically, but unlike the man opposite him he was eagerly awaiting his own release. With only two years service in the Metropolitan Police when the war started, there had been no objections when he sought permission to join up. He'd been commissioned in the same regiment as his father, but in view of his background, he had been seconded to military police duties. But at least he was doing a job he knew something about, which was unusual for the army. The irony of it was that he had learned more of criminal investigation in the army than he had done in his brief time in the civil police. But all that was soon to come to an end and he would be reporting back to the other Scotland Yard at the far end of Whitehall...as a constable.

'My corporal said that you wished to report a crime, Mr Weston.'

'Yes, sir.' There was no hesitation in Weston's clipped response. 'I reckon my platoon commander was murdered...in Normandy, sir.'

Pinder felt like saying that a hell of a lot of other people had been too, but Weston's intense attitude stemmed any such flippancy. The man was obviously serious. 'Perhaps you'd better tell me about it.'

'It was D-Day, sir. Sixth of June last year,' said Weston. Pinder nodded. 'We went ashore in almost the first wave. The battalion had been brought back from Italy, special like, and put to training in the New Forest.' He scoffed. 'Bloody clever that was. Anyone'd think we hadn't seen any action. Still, that's the army for you. My officer—Lieutenant Gibbons was his name—hadn't got no further than fifty yards up the beach when he went down—'

'I imagine that quite a few did.' Pinder spoke mildly.

Weston appeared to be on the verge of making a sharp retort, but his quick eye took in Pinder's string of campaign ribands. 'Aye, that's a fact, sir,' he said. 'Anyhow, I was first to him, despite the major.'

'Despite the major?'

'Company commander, sir. Bit of a madman, he was...begging your pardon, sir. Kavanagh. Major Kavanagh. Well, he shouted to leave Mr Gibbons, sir. Yelled something about the stretcher-bearers would take care of him, and to get on up the beach.'

'That's standard practice, surely?' Pinder was beginning to wonder what ex-Sergeant Weston was driving at.

'Yes, it is, sir, but the point was, I

didn't know why Mr Gibbons had gone down, sir. Jerry had loosed off a few as we came ashore, then he switched to the lads further down. Canadians, I think they were. And he never came back on us till after Mr Gibbons went down.'

Pinder leaned forward and put his elbows on the desk. 'What exactly are you saying, Mr Weston?'

'I think he was shot by one of his own, sir, not to put too fine a point on it.'

'Oh? And what makes you think that?'

'Well, me and Corporal Mooney—he was Number One Section corporal—we dragged Mr Gibbons up the beach to some bushes and left him there, even though the major was screaming to us to go on.'

'Yes.'

'Well, sir, we moved on about another hundred and fifty yards, well over the top by then, and that's when I got mine.' He nodded at his right arm. 'And I finished up in the same field ambulance as the one they'd taken Mr Gibbons to. So I had a chat with the medics like and they reckoned that he'd been dead on arrival.'

'Well, I still don't see—'

'As a result of being hit in the legs by machine-gun fire, sir. Reckon it had done his artery and he'd bled to death.'

'Well then—'

'But when Corporal Mooney and me had dragged him up the beach, sir, there weren't nothing wrong with his legs. He definitely hadn't been hit in the legs then.'

'Then perhaps he was hit after you'd left him in the bushes.'

Weston nodded confidently. 'I'm sure he was, sir, but I reckon he was already dead when Mooney and me dragged him away. And Mooney reckoned so too. The point was, there weren't no enemy fire on our bit of the beach when Mr Gibbons went down, sir.'

Pinder nodded slowly. 'I understand what you're saying, Mr Weston, but you can't be absolutely certain that Gibbons was dead when you left him, can you?'

Weston raised his chin slightly and looked at the military policeman for a second or so. 'I was in the retreat from Dunkirk, sir. And I went right through the Western desert...as far as second Alamein.' He nodded briefly towards Pinder's Africa Star riband. 'And that's to say nothing of the Sicily landing.' He paused. 'Reckon I can tell a dead 'un all right, sir. Seen enough of 'em.'

'Maybe so,' said Pinder, 'but even if it's true, it would be almost impossible to investigate. It would be very difficult to prove now, nearly a year later, that Gibbons did not die as a result of enemy action. Apart from anything else, tracing witnesses would be a mammoth task in itself.'

Weston pulled out his wallet and balanced it on his knees. He handled it awkwardly, obviously not yet used to using his left hand for everything, and took out a slip of paper. 'There you are, sir,' he said, pushing it across the desk towards Pinder. Then he recited the names from memory. 'Apart from Major Kavanagh, there was Captain Winters—he was the company 2IC; Corporal Mooney, of course, and his number two, Lance-Corporal Burton. Then there was the riflemen, "Tug" Wilson, Herbert, Murphy and "Knocker" White.' Weston grinned at Pinder. 'I got someone to write them down for me while I was in the hospital,' he said. 'But if you get in touch with them, they'll remember a few other names, no doubt.'

Pinder picked up the piece of paper and leaned back in his chair. 'So, Mr Weston, in the heat of the greatest invasion ever, you think that your platoon commander was murdered by one of his own men. And you want me to investigate it?'

'Yes, sir. Absolutely.'

'Well it's certainly an interesting little problem,' said Major Ford. He crossed his legs and tapped lightly on his desk-top with a paper-knife. Ford was one of the quaintly-styled Military Deputies of the Judge Advocate General's Department at the War Office. In other words, he was an army lawyer. And he was just as pernickety as most other lawyers that Pinder had met. 'I suppose that one could say,' he went on, 'that the venue of your alleged offence was French territory once more. Although the fact that the Germans had not officially ceded it might make a difference. On the other hand, we never officially recognised that it was ever other than French territory.'

'I'm a policeman, sir,' said Pinder, 'and all I want to know is if I discover that Gibbons was murdered by a British soldier, can I arrest him and bring him to trial...by court martial.'

'Yes...' said Ford slowly.

'Yes, I can?'

'No, I mean, yes I see the problem.' Ford reached for the *Manual of Military Law* and spent a few minutes skimming through it. 'I think your best bet is to go ahead, and if it seems likely that you have a suspect, we'll have to talk again, Captain Pinder.'

'Thank you, sir,' said Pinder, trying hard to keep any trace of sarcasm out of his voice.

'What does the Provost Marshal think about it, as a matter of interest?'

'He's ordered preliminary enquiries...and suggested speaking to you.'

Ford smiled. 'Yes,' he said again. 'Well, good luck. Don't envy you, quite frankly. Sounds as though it'll take ages.'

'Probably hold up my release, too,' said Pinder sourly.

The battalion of the Middlesex Rifles that ex-Sergeant Weston had belonged to was in Germany. In what was left of Cologne.

Major Kavanagh, the officer who had commanded Weston's company in the Normandy landings, was clearly a man who disliked policemen—military or civil,

Pinder imagined—and was extremely un-helpful. 'I've never heard such a cock-and-bull yarn in all my life, Captain Pinder,' he said, 'and I'm amazed that you got taken in by it.'

'An allegation has been made, sir,' said Pinder stiffly, 'and the Provost Marshal has ordered an investigation.' He remained standing in Kavanagh's office. The major had not invited him to sit down, nor had he sat down himself.

Kavanagh scoffed. 'He's obviously never met Weston,' he said, and paused. 'But you have.'

'He seemed a sincere man to me,' said Pinder.

'So he might be, but he was a fool.' Kavanagh balanced his swagger cane vertically on his desk with his hands on top and leaned his chin on them. 'Weston was a sergeant at the outbreak of war...a sergeant with twelve years regular service. Most of it in India, I may say. And at the end of the war, he was still a sergeant. But many regulars, those with anything about them, had been commissioned, and those who weren't quite top drawer as you might say, were certainly regimental sarn't-majors. Take Bob Winters for example. A

189

regular colour-sarn't when it all started, but finished up a captain. Speaks for itself, don't you think?'

'The fact that Weston remained a sergeant throughout the war—'

'Oh, he didn't,' interrupted Kavanagh. 'He was a company sarn't-major at one time, but got reduced for inefficiency...at my instigation.'

'That doesn't necessarily cast any doubt on his testimony, sir,' said Pinder. He disliked Kavanagh's pseudo regular-officer pose; he knew from his inquiries that Kavanagh had been a sports master at a second-rate public school when the war had started.

'Well, Captain Pinder, I was there, leading my company up the beach.' Kavanagh had sat down by now, and leaned back slightly so that Pinder could not fail to see that he had a Military Cross. 'And I saw Tony Gibbons go down. Bloody poor show. He was a good officer.' He leaned forward again. 'But so am I, Pinder, although I say it myself, and I was the chap who had to write to his parents. So I made bloody sure that I knew what had happened to him. The tragedy of it is, that if that fool Weston hadn't dragged him up the beach, he'd probably have been all right. As it happened, he got raked by MG fire where they left him and he bled to death from an artery.' Kavanagh stood up again, took a cigarette from a box on the desk and lit it, puffing nervously. 'And I must say that any suggestion that he was killed by one of his own men is...well, frankly, I find it not only incredible, but bloody insulting to the memory of a fine young officer.'

'Ex-Sergeant Weston told me that firing on your company had ceased when Gibbons fell, sir,' said Pinder.

'So you said, Pinder,' said Kavanagh acidly. 'So you said. And I'm telling you he made a mistake.'

'Nevertheless, sir, it is my intention to interview the other officers and soldiers who were there at the time.'

Kavanagh slowly exhaled cigarette smoke and gazed through it at the military police captain. 'I think what you mean, Captain Pinder, is that you would like my permission to interview some of the men under my command.'

Pinder had had enough. 'I'm not sure that you understand my remit, Major Kavanagh,' he said. 'I am conducting an enquiry on the express orders of the Provost Marshal...who is a major-general. I think that he would not be too pleased to learn that I was being obstructed in those enquiries.' Then he whipped one in under Kavanagh's guard. 'Nor, I suspect, would your colonel, to whom the PM's admonition would undoubtedly be addressed, sir.'

Kavanagh capitulated, petulantly. 'Talk to whoever you like, captain,' he said. 'It's your time and if you want to waste it, it's a matter for you.'

Unfortunately, Kavanagh was right. It was a complete waste of time.

Pinder interviewed all the men on Weston's list of so-called witnesses. Except two. Corporal Mooney had been killed in the Rhine crossing and Captain Robert Winters had been demobbed. He had secured an early release by standing for parliament in the general election of July 1945. But he had not been elected and was now the landlord of a pub somewhere near Stalybridge in Cheshire. Kavanagh's view was that Winters's lost deposit had been a cheap way of him getting out of the army sooner than everyone else.

It was a blow that Mooney had been

killed. From what Weston had said, he had been closer to Gibbons than anyone else, apart from Weston himself, and had helped to pull the unfortunate officer up the beach to the bushes.

Lance-Corporal Burton and the four riflemen were non-committal. Either that, or some ingrained fear of implication caused their memories to go blank as they always did whenever a military policeman asked them a question. They came up with a few names of other soldiers who had been near Lieutenant Gibbons when he fell, but they were no more helpful than the others.

It was August and in London the crowds were out again, this time celebrating the end of the war in the Far East. Pinder looked at the depressing pile of paper on a side table in his office. The investigation proper was no further forward. He picked up the phone and asked for an appointment with the Provost Marshal.

The paperwork had been unbelievable. To obtain permission for the exhumation of Lieutenant Gibbons's body from its temporary resting place near La Riviere, it seemed that Pinder had had to apply to just about every department at the War Office...and the Imperial War Graves Commission. But at last it was done and early on a chilly October morning, Pinder, several senior army officers and a captain in the Royal Army Chaplains' Department—why they were all there, Pinder never found out—foregathered to watch half a dozen pioneers dig up the makeshift grave.

Despite strong opposition, not least from the Provost Marshal himself, Pinder had succeeded in getting the body shipped back to England for examination by a Home Office pathologist.

Probably the most satisfying sound that Pinder ever heard was the metallic clink as the pathologist released the round from his tweezers and dropped it into an enamel bowl. 'I think that could be what you're looking for, captain,' he said. 'I don't know too much about guns, but even I can see that it's different from the rest.'

'And the cause of death?' asked Pinder hopefully.

'Oh that one, without a doubt.' The pathologist pointed with his tweezers. 'I think you said that the MO who examined this fellow said he'd died from arterial bleeding.'

'That's what I was told.'

'Well, he didn't. There was no excessive loss of blood from the leg wounds because he was already dead. Had been for some hours, I should think. But that little beauty...' He pointed at the odd round again. 'That was the one that did the damage. Through his back and straight into the heart. Couldn't be more fatal.' The pathologist grinned and peeled off his gloves. 'I don't blame the MO, mind you. Got his work cut out stitching up the wounded without wondering whether he's got a murder on his hands. Anyway, just because he's a doctor doesn't make him a pathologist.'

'Those,' said the ballistics expert at Scotland Yard, indicating the seven or eight rounds that been taken from Gibbons's legs, 'are 7.92 millimetre, probably fired from a German MG42.' He glanced up at Pinder. 'Very widely used by the Germans, they were. But this one...' He took a glass and examined the round taken from Gibbons's heart. 'That little fellow is most likely a 7.62 millimetre.'

'Is that significant?' asked Pinder.

The ballistics officer reached across and took a reference book from a shelf near his bench. 'The only pistol I can think of...' he began slowly, searching for the right place in the book. 'Yes, A Tula-Tokarev 1930.' He glanced up. 'It's a Russian job and I'm pretty certain that it's the only pistol you'll find that fires a 7.62 round.' He closed the book and shrugged. 'Not that that's foolproof, of course. You'd probably get away with using a 7.62 in, say, a German Bergmann or an Austrian Mannlicher 1901...if there are any still about. They both take a 7.63. You find the pistol and I'll tell you if it fired that round. But that's your problem.' He grinned cheerfully. 'I've done my bit.'

The coroner at Uxbridge—the body had been landed at RAF Northolt—opened the inquest and promptly adjourned it. Now it was up to Pinder.

The preliminaries were over. This time Pinder took a hard-nosed sergeant-major from the army's Special Investigation Branch with him to Germany. A pre-war policeman in the City Centre Division of Manchester City Police, Ted Palmer knew what he was about. And Ted Palmer did not suffer fools gladly. Particularly jumped-up majors. And particularly when Ted Palmer had already been advised that his release was through and that in two months time he would be a detective sergeant in Manchester once more.

But he still practised the niceties of military etiquette and crashed to attention with a quivering salute when he and Pinder were shown into Major Kavanagh's office.

'So you're back,' said Kavanagh, acknowledging the military policemen's salutes with a languid wave of his hand. 'What now?'

'This is Company Sar'nt-Major Palmer of the SIB, sir,' said Pinder. 'He is assisting me in my investigations into the murder of Lieutenant Gibbons.'

Kavanagh raised his eyebrows and glanced from Pinder to Palmer and back again. 'What on earth are you talking about? I thought I'd made it plain that—'

'I have the report of a Home Office pathologist in my briefcase, sir,' said Pinder, 'which proves to my satisfaction that Gibbons was shot in the back, prior to his being struck by the machine-gun rounds that were originally thought to have caused his death.'

'Originally thought?'

'Yes, sir. The medical evidence is conclusive. Gibbons died as a result of a round entering his back and penetrating his heart.'

'But that's absurd. Who the hell would want to kill Gibbons. He was a fine young man.'

'That, Major Kavanagh, is what we are here to find out.' It was the first time that Palmer had spoken, and his Mancunian accent grated on Kavanagh's ear.

'I see.' Kavanagh stood up and stared out of the window. Then he turned. 'Well, what d'you want of me?'

'An office, sir,' said Palmer,' where Captain Pinder and I can interview everyone in the company who took part in the Normandy landings.'

Kavanagh bridled at that. 'These men are busy, Sarn't-major,' he said. 'Part of the army of occupation. I'm not sure that it will be possible—'

'In that case, sir,' said Palmer, 'perhaps you would be so good as to direct me to your cypher room.'

'What for?'

'In order that I can send a signal to the Provost Marshal, sir, seeking further orders.'

Kavanagh shrugged and pushed his hands into his pockets. 'See the chief clerk,' he said. 'There's plenty of room here. He'll allocate you something.'

'Thank you, sir,' said Pinder, 'but while we're here, perhaps we can start with you.'

Kavanagh sank into his chair. 'As you wish. But I don't know what you expect me to tell you...that I haven't already told you, that is.'

'Was anyone in your company in possession of unauthorised weapons, sir?' asked Palmer.

A tired smile crossed Kavanagh's face. 'Dozens, I should think...'

Palmer frowned. 'Oh?'

'Er, not to my knowledge, of course,' said Kavanagh hurriedly. 'But you know what soldiers are. Always collecting souvenirs. There's been a General Routine Order about it, as you probably know, forbidding the practice, but...' He shrugged again.

'The same GRO requires officers to take positive steps to ensure that their men do not possess such weapons, sir,' said Palmer. 'Have you done so?'

'Of course, sarn't-major,' said Kavanagh icily. 'But for future reference, I do not tolerate being questioned on my responsibilities by a subordinate rank...even a CSM in the Corps of Military Police.'

'Quite so, sir,' said Palmer. 'And I shall not tolerate obstruction into a murder investigation...from anyone.'

'I presume that you are talking about the possession of unauthorised weapons at the time we came ashore at Gold Beach?' Kavanagh realised that there was little to be gained from alienating this abrasive warrant officer.

'Yes, sir.'

'In that case, I would say that it was extremely unlikely. Their kit was checked prior to embarkation, to make sure that they were carrying the equipment they needed. If any unauthorised weapons had been found, they would have been confiscated.'

'And the officers, sir?'

'What about them?'

'Was their kit checked?'

'Of course not. Officers are put on their honour.'

'Did you have any unauthorised weapons yourself, sir?' asked Palmer.

'I shall treat that question with the contempt it deserves, sarn't-major,' said Kavanagh.

'May be so, sir, but perhaps you'd answer it.'

'I had no unauthorised weapons in my possession,' said Kavanagh stonily.

Palmer took off his web belt and laid it carefully on the window ledge. 'We could take the simple view, sir,' he said, 'and assume it had to be an officer because the other ranks had been searched...'

'But?'

Palmer grinned. 'But I'm not buying it, sir.'

Pinder nodded. 'Neither am I, Ted. So where do we go from here?'

'Where we go from here, sir, is to put the arm on these lairy bloody squaddies. Put the fear of Christ up 'em. Someone'll talk, or I don't deserve to have this on my sleeve.' He put a finger on the woven crown on his cuff.

Pinder sat back and watched Palmer at work as, one after the other, he interviewed the remaining members of the company

201

in which Lieutenant Gibbons had served as a platoon commander. But it was a frustrating and inconclusive task. Some of the soldiers had died, either at Normandy or later, while others had been wounded or discharged from the army.

Then came a little light. Lance-Corporal Burton, who had been a member of Gibbons's platoon, started off by being as reticent as he had been when Pinder had interviewed him previously.

But Palmer was having none of it. 'Look here, lad—' he began.

'I'm not a lad, sir,' said Burton, standing on his dignity, 'I'm a lance-corporal—'

Palmer slapped the table with the flat of his hand. 'Don't you bloody come King's Regulations with me, laddie, or we'll continue this interview in the guardroom. Now then, I know that you know something, and I want to know what it is. And I'm not talking about thieving out of the Q Stores either. I'm talking about the murder of an officer.'

Lance-Corporal Burton took rapid stock of the situation and decided that it would be in his own interest not to come the old soldier with this military police warrant officer. 'He were a toffee-nosed little bugger,' he said, shooting a sideways glance at Pinder. 'Hoity-toity and full of hisself. You'd a-thought he were a general, way he carried on. When we was in training in the New Forest, he were always on about cleaning kit. Polishing buttons and boots, an' all that. Made a right pain of hisself, he did. And him a bloody prefect at school not ten minutes afore, I shouldn't wonder.'

Palmer did not want to deflect Burton from his theme and refrained from pointing out that Gibbons had been twenty-five years of age when he was killed. 'Not very popular among the lads, then? Is that the strength of it?'

'Aye, that an' more, sir,' said Burton. 'He were bloody detested, and if you're telling me that someone did for him when we came ashore, then I for one wouldn't be surprised. Nor sorry, neither.'

'Would you have done for him, given the chance, corporal?' asked Palmer mildly.

Burton grinned. 'I'd have happily given him a bunch of fives, sir,' he said, 'but I'm not daft enough to have shot him and then come here and say what I've just said. That'd be daft, that would.'

'Yes,' said Palmer. 'It would, wouldn't it. Well, who might have done? Was there anyone who'd particularly got it in for him? Someone who'd finished up with a fair amount of jankers...or a spell in the glasshouse, perhaps?'

'Corporal Mooney,' said Burton without hesitation. 'Bloody Gibbons got him busted. That were when we was in the New Forest, training. Took him in front of the colonel for insubordination and had him stripped. Mind you, he soon got made up again. Regular, Charlie Mooney were, and a good NCO. Bloody difficult to come by in wartime. As a matter of fact, Gibbons had a hell of a row with Captain Winters about it.'

'What sort of row?'

'Winters told him he was a jumped-up little sod, and that he didn't know a good soldier when he saw one. And he told Gibbons that he'd better mend his ways or he might find himself in trouble when it came to a bit of action.'

'What sort of trouble?' Palmer's eyes narrowed.

'He didn't rightly say, sir.'

'Hadn't Mr Gibbons been in action with the battalion before then?'

'No, sir.' Burton sniffed. 'One of the reinforcements he were, to make up the battalion strength when we got back from Italy. As far as I could tell, he'd been loafing about at the training depot. Normandy was the first time he'd seen a shot fired in anger, even though he'd been in from about 1940. Someone said he'd been a shiny-arse for a few years before he got commissioned, but I don't know whether that's true.'

Pinder had been glancing through Gibbons's record of service while Burton had been talking. The dead officer had come down from university in 1940 and had been commissioned the moment he entered the army. Obviously Burton's story about his having been a clerk was a piece of malicious gossip, the sort of tale that soldiers tended to spread to discredit an unpopular officer. Prior to the entry of Gibbons's death in action, there was a note that he had been recommended for—and was awaiting—promotion to captain.

'This row...between Captain Winters and Mr Gibbons. How come you knew about it, Corporal Burton?' asked Palmer.

'Bloody heard it, sir. Everyone did I should think. We was under canvas in the New Forest...' Burton grinned. 'That shook a few of 'em, I can tell you. Anyhow,

Captain Winters and Gibbons had a set-to outside the company office tent, just after Gibbons had got back from CO's orders, the day Charlie Mooney got busted down. And Captain Winters had a right go at him. Eventually, Major Kavanagh come out and broke it up. Gave the pair of 'em a bollocking for carrying on in front of the men.'

'And was that the end of it... I mean as far as Captain Winters and Mr Gibbons were concerned?'

Burton shrugged. 'Don't rightly know, sir. But there was always a bit of needle between 'em after that. You could tell. The captain usually called all the subalterns by their first name, except for Gibbons. An' he always called him *Mister* Gibbons, sarcastic like.'

'Corporal Mooney was one of the NCOs who dragged Mr Gibbons up the beach after he was hit, wasn't he?' asked Pinder.

Burton switched his gaze to the captain. 'That's right, sir. And Sarn't Weston were t'other.'

'Well, that doesn't sound like the action of a man who hated Mr Gibbons.'

'S'different, sir, ain't it. I mean when one of your own goes down you do what you can for him. Even if you do hate his guts.' Burton frowned slightly as though baffled that the military police officer could not follow this soldierly logic.

Major Kavanagh shrugged it off. 'You can hardly expect a lance-corporal to know of the relationship between officers. Yes, it's true that I had to intervene between Winters and Gibbons. Winters felt very strongly about the men and he objected to the way Gibbons exercised discipline. But Gibbons was right. If an NCO is insubordinate to an officer, then there's only one course of action...and on that occasion, he took it. Bob Winters, on the other hand, was a regular colour-sarn't when war broke out. I think I told you that.' Kavanagh raised an eyebrow and Pinder nodded. 'He had a different approach. If he had any trouble with his chaps, not that he often did, he'd invite them to the gym to put the gloves on. Not a course of action I approved of, but that was Bob Winter's way. And the men loved him for it. After all, when you're leading men into action, you've got to have their whole-hearted loyalty.'

'What about Corporal Mooney, major?'

asked Pinder. 'It's been suggested that he had it in for Gibbons as a result of Gibbons getting him reduced in rank.'

Kavanagh shook his head. 'Mooney got what he deserved, and he knew it. He was a regular soldier, after all. He knew the rules. Anyway, he got made up again shortly afterwards. I think he was a rifleman only for about two weeks. Couldn't afford to lose an NCO like him. But we did unfortunately...at the Rhine crossing.'

Once Company Sergeant-Major Palmer had heard what Lance-Corporal Burton had said about Lieutenant Gibbons, he tackled the other soldiers afresh. The second time they were interviewed, they agreed with Burton about Gibbons's unpopularity, and a few had been witness to the shouting match between him and Captain Winters. But that was as far as Palmer got.

'Well, Ted, where are we?' asked Pinder.

'In Cologne, sir,' said Palmer, 'but we ought to be in Stalybridge, talking to ex-Captain Winters.' He looked up from the file and grinned. 'Not far from my old stamping ground that.'

'It's *Mr* Winters...or Bob, if you prefer. I dropped the captain bit when I took this pub. Doesn't carry much weight with the locals round here, I can tell you. What did you want?'

'Wanted to talk to you about Lieutenant Gibbons,' said Pinder.

'Better come into the back room,' said Winters and led the way through a door off the private bar.

The room was part sitting room, part office, and Winters waved a hand at a woman seated at a roll-top desk. 'This is Cathy, my wife,' he said. 'These gentlemen are from the military police,' he added.

Cathy Winters was about twenty-five and exuded sex-appeal. Her hair-style had been copied straight from *Moviegoer* magazine and she wore a white sweater that accentuated her curves. She blew cigarette smoke in the air and smiled. 'Hallo,' she said.

'Have a pew,' said Winters, indicating a settee with a sweep of his hand. 'Now what's this about Tony Gibbons?'

'I'm investigating his death,' said Pinder. There seemed no point in skirting round the reason for his visit.

'Well, that shouldn't be a problem, old

209

boy.' Winters sat down and reached across in front of his wife to take a packet of cigarettes from the desk. 'Tony Gibbons was killed in the Normandy landings,' he said, once he had lit a cigarette. 'Sorry, do you?' He offered the packet to Pinder and Palmer. 'I was there, and Tony was killed the minute he hit the beach.'

'But not by enemy action,' said Pinder. 'He was murdered.'

'What the hell are you talking about?' Winters stared at the military policeman.

'His body has been exhumed and a round from what we believe to be a Russian pistol was taken from his heart,' said Pinder. 'He was shot in the back. A lucky shot, too, given that he was wearing a small pack at the time.'

'Christ!' said Winters. 'That's bloody incredible. I won't ask you if you're sure, you obviously are, but what you're saying is that one of our blokes killed him, is that it?'

'Possibly.'

'But who in hell's name would have wanted...?' Winters left the sentence unfinished and shook his head slowly.

'I understand that you and Mr Gibbons

didn't exactly see eye to eye, Mr Winters,' said Palmer.

Winters looked up sharply. 'Now hold on, old boy,' he said. 'He wasn't exactly my cup of tea, if that's what you mean, but if you think that I had anything—'

'What exactly annoyed you about him?'

'Had too good an opinion of himself for my liking.' Winters stood up and walked across the room to a sideboard. 'Scotch?' he asked, glancing over his shoulder.

Pinder shook his head. 'Too early for me, thanks, but don't let me stop you.'

'You won't,' said Cathy Winters drily, and stubbed out her cigarette.

'We had a few exchanges, but that was inevitable, I suppose,' said Winters, sitting down again and taking a sip of his whisky. 'There were a lot like him. In the army five minutes, and think they know it all.'

'It was a bit longer than that,' said Pinder. 'He was commissioned in 1940.'

Winters shrugged. 'So? I was a colour-sergeant with seven years service when the war started. But Gibbons came straight into the officers' mess...and thought he knew it all. You can't treat men the way he did and get away with it.'

'Meaning?'

'Meaning that when you take men into action, you've got to make sure they follow you because they've got confidence in your leadership. With Gibbons they did as they were told because they were more frightened of him than they were of the enemy. That's no way to do it. And I know. Don't forget I'd seen it from both sides. When you're a ranker, you know what it's like to have had an idiot for an officer. And Gibbons was an idiot.'

'There was a rather public row between the two of you about a Corporal Mooney, I understand.'

'It wasn't a row. I was a captain and he was a lieutenant. I tore him off a strip, bloody fool. When you're waiting to embark for an invasion, the men are tense. You have to make allowances for it. You don't run them in front of the old man because they answer you back. No, old boy, I gave him a bollocking. Well deserved, too.'

'Major Kavanagh told me that he intervened.'

Winters took another sip of Scotch and grinned. 'Yeah, he did. Quite right, I suppose. Not the done thing for one officer to ball out another in front of the men, but I'm afraid he made me see red. Mooney was a bloody good soldier. I'll give you that he was a bit lippy, but he never tried it on with me. That's the test, you see. That's the gauge of an officer. The men can tell the good from the bad.'

'As far as you were concerned then, he was an officer who needed pulling into line from time to time.'

'All the time, rather than from time to time, but yes, that's about the strength of it.'

'I'm also told that you always called him Mr Gibbons, rather than Tony.'

'Who told you that?'

'An NCO,' said Pinder.

Winters scoffed. 'Well, he would. You're always formal in front of the men, but we called each other by first names in the mess...except for the colonel.' He paused. 'Well, you know the form, for Christ's sake.'

'Do you know of anyone, officer or soldier, who possessed an unauthorised weapon, Mr Winters? Who might have had one, or could have had one, when you went ashore on Gold Beach?'

Winters shook his head. 'No chance, old boy. The men had their kit searched, and anyone who was found with such a weapon would have been in trouble.'

'What about the officers? Were they searched?'

'Mine were,' said Winters. 'Kavanagh burbled on with some rubbish about putting the officers on their honour, but I was having none of that. Went through their kit, same as the men.'

'But Major Kavanagh's kit was not examined...by the colonel, for instance?'

Winters laughed outright. 'Have you met the colonel?'

Pinder shook his head. 'Different colonel when we got there. The officer who'd been CO at Normandy had gone. At the War Office now, so I'm told.'

Winters laughed again. 'Best place for him. Had all the traditions of the old Indian Army, he did. Officers and gentlemen, and all that crap. Couldn't come to terms with the fact that the officers' mess was half full of scoundrels. Car salesmen, bank clerks...there was even a bloody taxi-driver.' Winters paused. 'But at least they had the sense to make him mechanical transport officer.'

Pinder looked at the calendar on his desk.

Another twenty-two days and he could be out of the army and back to the Metropolitan Police. He wondered if that was the right thing to do. For nearly seven years he had known nothing but soldiering, and he wondered whether he should stay. The offer had been made, but he was wavering still, even though the prospect of walking a beat, at all hours and in all weathers, was not as good a job as the one he had now. Ted Palmer was long gone, back to Manchester and now a detective inspector. The one thing that rankled was the failure of his enquiry into the death of Lieutenant Gibbons. Despite all the work that he and Ted Palmer had done, they had got nowhere. But Palmer, the realist, with all that CID experience behind him, had not held out much hope to start with.

Pinder stood up and opened the window. The sound of distant bands heralded the start of the Victory Parade, a year and a month after VE Day. And a year and a month since ex-Sergeant Weston had walked in to make the allegation that had started it all off.

'Excuse me, sir.' The chief clerk stuck his head round the door.

215

'What is it, staff?'

'Lady to see you, sir.' The staff-sergeant grinned. 'Bit of all right, too.'

Pinder frowned. Although his fiancée, a BEA stewardess, called in from time to time, she should have been in Paris right now. 'Who is it, staff?'

'A Mrs Winters, sir. Says it's important.'

She was wearing a blue dress with a full skirt, and high heels. 'Hallo, captain,' she said. She looked tired and drawn.

'Well, Mrs Winters. And what can I do for you?' Pinder walked round the desk and moved a chair for her.

'My husband was killed in a road accident last week.'

'Good God, how awful. I am sorry—' began Pinder.

Cathy Winters held up a hand. 'I won't weary you with the sordid details, Captain Pinder,' she said. 'But while Bob was in Italy, I was living in married quarters at the depot and Tony Gibbons was the assistant adjutant.' She glanced up at Pinder, briefly. 'We had an affair, a very torrid affair. I'm afraid we weren't too discreet about it either, and Bob got to know when he came home...just before the invasion. After his death, I found this

216

in his safety deposit box at the bank.'
She opened her handbag and laid a pistol
on Pinder's desk. It was a Tula-Tokarev
1930.

You May See a Strangler

Peter Lovesey

Helen's mind was made up. Three times today she had got to the point of picking up the phone to call the police. She had pressed the first two numbers of the emergency code, then stopped, her finger poised over the third. Some loss of nerve had impelled her to hang up.

This time she would not falter. She stretched out her hand.

The phone bleeped before she touched it. Reacting as if she had disturbed a snake, she backed against the wall.

Outside in Carpenter Avenue, the kids from next door were skateboarding. Bees were plundering the lavender bush. Her neighbour Sally walked by on her way to the art class. Sally modelled nude for five pounds an hour and thought nothing of it. She was Helen's closest friend, a free spirit, unencumbered by her four kids. Before the firstborn arrived, Sally had organised

219

a baby-sitting circle. Helen could discuss anything with her. Or almost anything. Cool, liberated Sally wouldn't fathom how any woman could be afraid to pick up a phone.

She braced herself. 'Yes?'

'Helen?'

'Speaking.'

'So you don't know who this is.' The voice was difficult to place. Female, youngish, with a trace of the north. There was background noise of voices laughing and talking animatedly, and music.

'I...I'm sorry. Your voice is familiar, but...'

'Come on, you can do better than that, love. Picture a blousy dame with pink-rimmed specs and a blonde pony-tail.'

She dredged the name from her troubled mind. 'Immy.' Imogen had been her mainstay through that dreary history course at university. 'It's over ten years. It must be.'

'Eleven this June since we chucked our course-notes into the Avon and got totally Brahms and Lizst. Remember? How are things with you, Helen? You don't sound too chipper from here.'

'It's nothing.'

'An off-moment? What's your news? I know there's a man in your life now. Nelson, am I right?'

'How do you know that?'

'From the Christmas card you sent one year. You caught me out. I didn't think we were the sort who sent cards.'

'That was the only year I sent.'

'Properly hitched, are you?'

'Yes.'

'Kids?'

'No.' Helen made an effort to switch the questioning. 'How about you, Immy? Did you marry?'

'Me? Can you imagine it? I lived with a footballer for a bit. He was the striker for Manchester City Reserves, whatever that means. All the training kept him really warm, specially on those freezing nights in January. Talk about cosy. I didn't use the electric blanket all winter. But he got sweaty when the weather improved so I blew the whistle. That's meant to be a joke, sweetie. You're supposed to fall about laughing.'

'Sorry.'

'You would have laughed in the old days. You *are* down. It isn't your health, is it?'

'I'm fine.' Helen was trying to decide whether this call from Imogen was just for the chat or whether a visit was imminent. In her present crisis she couldn't face doing the hostess bit, not even for Immy. 'Where are you calling from?'

'Got you worried, have I?' Imogen said, laughing.

'Of course not.'

'Go on—you've got a mental picture of me standing on your doorstep with two enormous suitcases and a dog.'

'Normally I'd love to see you, but—'

'It's all right, kiddo, you can relax. Put your feet up, wash your hair, have nookie with Nelson on the bearskin rug. I'm not about to descend on you.'

'You're just as daft as ever,' Helen said, trying to sound matey and not succeeding. 'Where *are* you speaking from? It sounds like a party there.'

'The mental picture gets worse—two suitcases and a dog, and a carload of drunks with funny hats. I said relax. There's no way I'm going to make a nuisance of myself.'

'The last I heard you were back in the north.'

'And so I am. Granadaland. Back to

my roots. I'm a television researcher. The history degree got me in, but I make sod all use of it. I don't know why they keep me on.'

Manchester. At least two hundred miles away. While Imogen was outlining the pleasures and perils of TV research, Helen's thoughts became less guarded. The voice from the past, chattering freely, confiding failure as readily as success, revived that time in their second year when they had opened their minds to each other. Talking to Immy had been a balm at that vulnerable stage of her life. She had kept nothing back.

Then wasn't this a God-sent opportunity? All the reason she had for not confiding in Sally next door didn't apply to Imogen. Immy was remote now, eleven years and two hundred miles away. Remote, yet close in spirit. A sympathetic ear. No, that wasn't the point—it wasn't sympathy she wanted. An understanding ear. Immy understood her. She might even know what to do.

'Now what about you, poppet?' Imogen ended by saying. 'What's your news?'

'Mine?' In her anguish Helen covered her mouth with her hand and pressed her

223

fingers into the flesh under her cheekbones.

'Helen, it's bloody obvious I must have got you at a difficult time,' Imogen said. 'Typical of me, wittering on like that. Look, I'll call you back another day.'

'No. No, I want to talk,' Helen managed to say. 'God knows, I want to talk. It must be fate that you called.'

Concern flooded into Immy's voice. 'Darling, what is it?'

Helen started by saying, 'What would you do if...?' and then switched to a blunt statement. 'Immy, I believe Nelson is a murderer.'

She heard the intake of breath from Imogen. The background voices shrilled and giggled inanely.

'I know it must sound crazy spoken cold like this. You must have seen all that stuff in the papers about the Surrey Strangler, the man who killed those women. I think it's Nelson.'

When—after another pause—the voice at the end of the phone responded, it was compassionate, but sceptical, with the tone of a mother attempting to coax the truth from her child. 'Helen, how do you know?'

Helen made an effort to sound rational.

Now that she'd confided her appalling suspicion she had to convince Immy that she was still sane. For a start she needed to convey something of Nelson's personality. She described how she had met him four years ago in the cinema queue for the latest James Bond, how he had offered to keep her place when the rain started tipping down, just when she was about to give up for the sake of her hair. He'd got drenched, along with the others who'd kept their positions, but she'd been able to shelter in the cinema entrance. And when they'd finally got their tickets he hadn't done the expected thing and used his gallantry as a ploy to sit beside her. (She was doing her best to be just to Nelson). He hadn't forced the pace of their relationship at all. He'd found a seat a couple of rows behind her and they'd only spoken in the foyer as they came out. She'd caught his eye and smiled and only then had he asked her to join him for a coffee in the pub across the street. That was how tentative his first approach had been.

'He isn't dishy, or anything. I mean, he isn't ugly, but you wouldn't look twice at him. He's about average height, dark, with a dent in his nose from falling off his bike when he was a boy. What appealed to me was his personality. Immy, he gave me this wide-eyed look—his eyes are brown, by the way—like he'd just arrived from another planet and never seen a woman before. It made me quite dopey. From the beginning he treated me like someone special, as if I was the first girl he'd ever known. He still does. That's what makes this so creepy. He's never hurt me, or anything, never been violent in any way. If we have a row, as everyone does from time to time, he just goes out of the room until we both see how ridiculous it is to fight.'

'What makes you think he...?' Immy declined to supply the rest.

'The dates, the places. Each of those women was killed within thirty miles of here. It's happened each time on a night when Nelson got in really late—I mean well after midnight. He spends ages in the bathroom showering—I hear the tank filling in the loft—and then he sleeps downstairs on the sofa. When I ask him about it in the morning he says he didn't want to disturb me after getting in so late.'

'Do you ask him why he got in late?'

'Clients, he says. He's a sales rep

for a firm that makes computer games. Sometimes he has to see people in the evenings.'

'Does he tell you which client he's been with? Maybe you could check in some way.'

'It's not so simple as that. He doesn't go in for talking about his work.'

'And you say all the dates fit?'

'Yes.'

'Listen, I never read things like that in the papers. How many women has this guy killed?'

'Three.'

'It could be coincidence. Has Nelson been out other evenings when a woman wasn't killed?'

'Never so late. Generally he's back by eleven at the latest. And he hardly ever takes a shower before going to bed.'

'But is that all you've got to go on? Just the dates? I mean, these poor women must have fought the guy who attacked them. They were raped as well as strangled, weren't they? Have you noticed scratches, marks, any signs?'

'There was a scratch down the side of his face a few months ago, but I can't say exactly when it got there. I didn't have these suspicions then. Nelson said he got clawed by a cat.'

'A cat?'

'In a pub. He picked it up and it scratched him.'

'Have you looked at his clothes? What about spots of blood, hairs and so on? Scent?'

'I tried to find his shirt last Wednesday, after that nurse was killed in Dorking. He got in terribly late, like the other times. Next morning when I heard on the radio what had happened, I looked in the laundry basket, feeling really sick at what I was doing, and found that the shirt he'd been wearing wasn't there. It wasn't in his room either. Nor were his underpants. I think he must have got rid of them somehow. They weren't in the rubbish sack. Immy, did you see the detective on the television news speaking about it? He said someone must be withholding information, someone who suspects that the man they live with could be this murderer. He said by remaining silent they could have the deaths of more women on their conscience. I've got to speak to them, haven't I?'

Imogen sidestepped the question. 'You

won't mind if I ask a personal question?'

'What is it? Go ahead.'

'What's the sex like with Nelson?'

Helen had always found it difficult to talk about such things. If anyone but Imogen had asked her that question she would have slammed down the phone. 'He's never tried to force me, if that's what you're getting at.'

'But you do allow him to make love to you?'

She saw the drift. 'I'm not frigid, for God's sake. I mean it was never *that* passionate, and when it happens it's sometimes more like a duty than a pleasure, or it is for me, but we do sleep together, yes.'

'So the satisfaction isn't there?'

'Did I say that? I suppose it's true.' Not for the first time, Helen found herself wondering whether she was partly to blame. She wasn't experienced or comfortable as a lover. She hadn't the confidence to be anything but passive. Since the latest episode she couldn't imagine herself wanting Nelson ever again.

Through the net curtains she could see the accountant who lived at the end house. He always got back from the city about this time. Several paces in the rear came his Vietnamese wife. Each day she walked to the station to meet him and trail respectfully home behind him, carrying his briefcase. Most couples' relationships aren't paraded so obviously.

'If you go to the police, that's the end of your marriage,' Imogen said. 'Even if he's totally innocent, the point is that you believed this ghastly thing was possible. That's a betrayal in itself.'

Helen was silent.

'Do you really want my advice, love?'

'Immy, I do.'

'You're sure he wouldn't hurt you?'

'He never has.'

'Then I think you owe it to Nelson to talk to him.'

'Tell him what I believe?'

'If I were faced with this, I hope I'd have the guts to do the same.'

'They issued one of those photofit pictures,' Helen said, shrinking from the advice. 'I don't think it looks much like him apart from his eyes and hair.'

'So you want to be certain, and the only way is to find out the truth from Nelson.'

She wavered. 'How can I say such a

terrible thing to him?'

'You mean you'd rather say it to the police?'

Inwardly, Helen admitted the truth of this. Until Immy had suggested confronting Nelson, such a course of action had been too hideous even to contemplate. The most she had been prepared to do was to turn Nelson in. Faced with the biggest crisis in her life she had looked for the easy solution, the coward's way.

'Where is he right now?' Imogen asked.

'Out on the road somewhere. He should be back in the next hour or so.'

'Then why don't you talk to him when he gets in? If he's innocent—and he could be—it's the only way to save your marriage, if that's what you want.'

'I don't know if I can face it.'

'You must, poppet, you must. You asked for my advice and that's it.' Having delivered it, Immy steered the call to an end with a promise that she would phone back next day to find out what had happened. Helen thanked her and managed to say that they must meet some time. She put down the phone.

It was seven-fifteen. Generally Nelson got in by eight. Immy had convinced her.

Helen started rehearsing what she would say. She could broach it indirectly, claiming that she'd looked for his pink shirt with the red stripes—the one he'd been wearing Tuesday—to put in the washing-machine. She could remind him that Tuesday was the night he'd got in really late. His responses might give him away. He might even be willing to talk about what had happened. If only it could be so simple...

The hour of eight passed. It was getting dark, but she didn't draw the curtains. She stood waiting, staring out of the window. A red Toyota like Nelson's slowed as if to stop, then turned into the drive of one of the neighbours.

She went to make herself some tea and realised when she handled the warm pot that she'd already had two mugs since Immy's call. She'd be awash with the stuff. Instead she did something quite out of character by going to the cupboard where they kept the drinks and pouring herself a gin and tonic. With growing intimations of dread she took up her vigil at the window again.

Another hour went by.

For distraction she dusted the surfaces in the front room, still in darkness, looking out intermittently for the gleam of headlights in the street. She dusted everything twice, moving the ornaments by touch, like a blind person.

It must have been getting on for ten when she heard the heavy tread of a man in the street. She couldn't see enough to tell if it was Nelson, but her pulse raced faster when she saw the shape of someone coming up the garden path. An explanation leapt into her brain: the car had broken down and he'd had to come home by train.

She waited for the sound of his key in the latch. What she heard instead was the doorbell. He was never without his key.

The light in the hall dazzled her when she switched it on. She blinked as she opened the door.

'Sorry to disturb you, Helen,' the man on the doorstep said.

He was the neighbour, Gerald. She stared at him blankly.

'I'm slightly puzzled,' he told her. 'Sally isn't back. She's always in by now. I wondered if she said anything to you about what she was doing tonight.'

Her thoughts had been so focused on Nelson that it was an effort to register

Sally's existence, let alone her movements that day. Finally she succeeded in saying, 'I thought she was modelling at the tech. I saw her go past at the usual time.'

'Have you spoken to her at all today?'

'Er—no.'

'Maybe she's gone for a drink with somebody in the class,' said Gerald. 'I wouldn't think twice about it normally, but you can't be too careful these days, you know?'

She gave a nod. She knew what was on his mind. There was no need to say more.

Gerald repeated his apology and left. After she'd closed the door, Helen wondered whether she should have offered to babysit, giving Gerald a chance to walk down to the tech and enquire about Sally. Maybe that had been his real reason for calling. She could have gone after him, but she didn't want to be out when Nelson got back. Besides, she told herself in justification, if Sally *was* having a drink with someone from the class, she might not be overjoyed at her husband turning up. Not that Sally was wayward; simply that she'd balk at being treated as if she were in moral danger.

If the unspeakable had happened, and Sally had met the strangler, what could Gerald do? What could anyone do?

More than three hours had passed since Helen had been on the point of calling the police about Nelson. The appalling thought occurred to her that if Sally had met Nelson as she was leaving the tech, she might easily have accepted a lift. Sally knew Nelson. She'd assume she was safe with him. The words of that detective on the television taunted Helen. *'Someone out there knows this man. By remaining silent, they put more women in danger. If they have any conscience at all they should come forward and prevent another murder.'*

Instead of listening to Immy, she should have spoken to the police. Immy had been wrong, catastrophically wrong. She hadn't considered the possibility that if Nelson was the strangler he might kill again tonight.

But it was wrong to blame Immy. The responsibility was her own. She, Helen, should have sensed the dangerous flaw in the advice.

Nelson finally got in at ten to one. He hadn't abandoned the car, apparently. He closed the garage doors quietly—furtively,

Helen thought—and let himself in. He was clearly startled when she turned on the light.

'I thought you'd be in bed.'

'I thought I'd wait,' she said in a flat voice.

'Is something the matter?'

'You tell me, Nelson. Look at you. Your hand is bleeding.'

Two long scratches were scored across the back of his right hand. He covered them with his left. His tie was twisted askew and there were buttons missing from his shirt-front. 'I need a drink,' he said.

She followed him into the front room and watched him help himself from the whisky bottle.

'You haven't even pulled the curtains,' he remarked. It seemed to matter to him that they should not be seen from the street. His right hand went up to the cord and tugged at it, displaying the scratches.

Helen said, 'I was looking out for you. I didn't expect you to be so late.'

'I can't predict what's going to happen.'

She found herself saying, 'Maybe a psychiatrist could.'

The hunted look that was already in Nelson's eyes gave way first to horror, then, unexpectedly, to tears. He bowed his face and covered it with his hands. He was sobbing.

Helen had no need of her strategies, the questions about the times he'd been late before, and the missing clothes. She had tapped the truth.

And now she had to find out all of it. She still felt safe with him; some instinct told her that he wouldn't attack her, whatever he'd done to those other women. 'Where is she, Nelson? Where did you leave her?'

He said in a broken voice, 'The river, in the park.'

'Ashdown Park?'

He nodded, still sobbing. The local park was just a ten minute walk away. Sally's children played there often.

'Is she dead?'

'Yes.' After a pause he added, 'You're right—I'm mentally ill. I was locked up for six years before I met you. I should have told you.'

Stunned, she still knew that he was telling the truth. She understood why he'd so often stared at her as if she belonged to another species. She'd allowed herself to be flattered instead of sensing what that wide-eyed regard really meant.

Nelson said, 'I'm going to call the police. I've been wanting to call them. Believe me, I planned to call them. That's why I did it so close to home tonight. I was making sure they'd get me, if you can understand.'

She took the phone to him and waited while he dialled the number and spoke. He told them who he was and where he lived and what he had done. Then he replaced the phone and told Helen, 'They're sending a car.'

She said, 'I knew it was you. I should have turned you in. I'm always going to blame myself. How could you, Nelson, knowing she had four young children?'

He looked at her without a spark of comprehension. 'Who?'

'Sally.'

'Sally?'

'Sally next door.'

'What are you talking about? It wasn't Sally,' he said. 'It was some north country woman staying in the King's Arms. That's where I picked her up.'

Helen registered first that Sally was spared; she must after all have gone out with some people from the art class.

Then she played Nelson's words over in her mind. 'This woman—what did she look like?'

'About your age. Blonde hair and glasses. She didn't know the town. She was something in television. Said she was at a loose end tonight. She'd planned to drop in on an old college friend, only it wasn't convenient.'

The Curtain with the Knot in It

Shena Mackay

'You can see my window from here. It's the one with the curtain with the knot in it.'

Alice shivered, although the April late afternoon sun was turning the day room of Daffodil Ward into a greenhouse.

'Goose walked over your grave.' Pauline gave her abrupt laugh.

Alice looked out reluctantly across to the staff residential block, a three-storeyed cube of mottled brick, and located a dull curtain tied in a knot at a top floor window.

Why, she wondered, had she shuddered like that? Was it the knot? Or the intimation that Pauline the Domestic had a life beyond Daffodil?

Pauline laughed again, at the antics of Jack, one of the patients, who had almost managed to slide under the tray that confined him to his chair.

241

'Come on Jack Be Nimble, Jack Be Quick,' she said as she pulled him back. 'You'll be having your soup in a minute.'

If a copy were to laugh, Alice thought, or did she mean a capybara? Something with unattractive teeth and lank fur, unpopular with visitors at the zoo. The two women were of an age and dressed similarly, but with a world of difference between Alice's tracksuit and trainers and what was visible of Pauline's; pinkish-white and greyish-white peeking from under her nylon gingham overall. Pauline's hair hung limply from a rufflette of brown and yellow gingham, while Alice's was in a longish shiny bob.

Ada had been shouting from her chair for the curtains to be pulled since the rain had stopped and the sun had appeared two hours earlier, and now Sister was exasperated into swiping out spring with a swish of the orange curtains.

Alice's father had been wheeled into the ward so that something could be done to him, so she sat on a massive vinyl chair attempting to read a Large Print book whose pages had been glued together with Complan. Pauline went about her work, tearing sheets of pale blue paper from a large roll and slapping them down at each place on the long table, and on the trays of the chairs where the immobile were propped up on lolling and slipping pillows. Supper would not be served for an hour, but those who could Zimmer themselves there or who could be yanked and hoisted were seated at the table. Children's BBC blared on the television.

Anybody familiar with the tragedies, the dramas, the macabre comedies played out daily in places such as Daffodil, and the boredom, the cross-purpose nature of every exchange will need no description at supper time in this nursery of second childhood. Suffice it to say that it was a Wednesday and the big wooden calendar read Sunday, that the two budgies, presented by a well-wisher after the goldfish's suicide, twittered unregarded, a voice called incessantly 'help me, help me, somebody please help me'; the never-opened piano and record player were there, and the floral displays in beribboned baskets, faded to the colour and texture of Rice Krispies, and in the side ward people who had died long ago were cocooned in cots and tended as if they might, some day, hatch into something marvellous, or exude skeins of wonderful silk.

When it became apparent that Dad had been put to bed, Alice went to say goodnight to him.

'Don't know why you bother coming every day,' said Pauline. 'He doesn't know you from a bar of soap, nemmind though, I've got a soft spot for your Dad myself.'

She was pouring powdered soup into the orange plastic beakers from an aluminium jug. George was spooning out his reconstituted bits of mushroom and laying them neatly on his blue paper. Mrs Rosenbaum didn't want any soup because she was dead.

'Aren't you staying for your tea tonight?' Pauline asked Alice.

'No, I'd better be going. Got a lot to do at home.'

She felt unequal to the nice milky one, two sugars, tonight. A misunderstanding early in their relationship made it impossible now for her to explain that she liked her tea black and unsweetened. 'I look after my *friends.*' Pauline would say darkly, with a pointed glanced at Dolly's daughter who had unwittingly offended and was not allowed tea. Alice's worst fear was that Dad would not die before Pauline's, as yet unspoken but looming, invitation to an off-duty cuppa in her flat.

Croxted Memorial, originally a cottage hospital, was built to a strange hexagonal design, with a small Outpatients and Casualty tacked on to one side, and even after a year of visiting, Alice could get lost, take a wrong turning and end up where she started or at the dead end of the permanently locked Occupational Therapy, or the kitchens with their aluminium vats and trolleys. The grey floor gleamed, with little bubbles of disinfectant, a sign that read *Cleaning in Progress* half blocked her path, as it did every day although there were so few visitors or staff around that the place was like a morgue in the evenings, and there was Kevin the cleaner, leering over the handle of his heavy-duty polisher, pallied as a leek with a tangle of pale dirty roots for hair. She knew she should have taken the other exit.

'Off out somewhere nice, are we?'

She gave a smile which tried to be enigmatic, distancing and hinting at a world beyond his overalls and disinfectant.

'When you coming out with me then?'

Alice pulled out her diary and flicked through the pages, aware of him squirming with incredulous lubricity.

'Let me see, I think I'm free on the twelfth.'

'You what...'

'Yes. The Twelfth of Never.' She snapped the diary shut triumphantly.

That was cruel, Alice. She admonished herself as she inhaled healing nicotine and evening air after the dead atmosphere which was Pauline's and Kevin's element, standing on the ashphalt marled with white blossom while a blackbird sang in a cherry tree. Still, Kevin's idea of a venue for a good night out was probably that dark place behind the boiler room, where the wheelie bins lived.

Alice had lied to Pauline about having things to do, and deceived Kevin. The pages of her diary were almost all blank. Since she had been made redundant her world had shrunk until Daffodil and the long journeys by foot and tube and bus were her whole life. She no longer thought of herself as Alice at the Mad Hatter's tea party nearly as often as she had in the beginning. Her father, a Detective Inspector struck down and withered by illness over the years, was all the family she had and she loved him and grieved for his plight. She did not cry tonight; she had cried in so many hospital car parks over the years.

Kevin watched her from the doorway, drawing deeply on a pinched roll-up. His glance went up to a window with a knotted curtain, billowing, deflated, in the wind that had sprung up, ruffling his hair.

Inside, in Daffodil, Pauline ruffled George's white hair as she collected his dishes.

'All right, Georgie Porgie?'

Writhing in agony from the pressure sore that was devouring him like an insatiable rodent, he drew back his lips in what Pauline took to be a smile.

'Pudding and Pie,' she added.

'You haven't eaten your sandwiches,' she accused Mrs Rosenbaum, whipping away the three triangles of bread and ham. When she had been brought in Mrs Rosenbaum had tried to explain about eating kosher, but none of the staff or agency nurses had been able to take it on board, and she had shrunk into silence under her multi-coloured crochet blanket, while her feet swelled in the foam rubber boots fastened with velcro that Physio had provided, as slow starvation took its course.

The commodes that doubled as transport up the wooden hill to Bedfordshire were rolling into the day room.

'Come on Mary, Mary Quite Contrary,' said Sister Connelly as two of the Filipinos, they all looked the same to Pauline, and they never spoke to her anyway, started loading Mary on board. Quacking away in Foreign like a load of mandarin ducks. Thank God it was nearly time to knock off. She was really cheesed off today. Ada was singing, if you could call it that, 'Ere we are again, 'Appy as can be. All good pals and JOLLY...' she always got stuck there.

'Change the record, Ada!' Pauline shouted as Ada started up again.

'Pack it in, Joey. I've got a headache.' She told the budgies.

'Noisy buggers!'

'What are their names?' Alice had asked her once.

'I call them Joey. Can't tell them apart.' Pauline had replied.

'One's more emerald and the other's more turquoise.'

'You don't have to clear up after them!' It was all right for some people with nothing better to do to go all soppy over a pair of budgies.

'I know why the caged bird sings,' Alice had said, but before she could go on Jack had tipped his chair over. Alice had had to sign a form as a witness to show that there had been no negligence, after the doctor had been called, but that was the last they heard of the matter.

Outside at last, Pauline had an impulse to take off her trainers and walk barefoot over the daisies in the grass, but Kevin was lurking around so she didn't. A blackbird was singing in the cherry tree, black against the white blossom. Pauline stood still for a moment, then, 'I've got a lot to do at home,' she said to herself and headed for the concrete stairs that led up to her flat. It was her thirty-seventh spring. Later that evening she went down to the payphone and dialled a number. She knew it by heart; it had stuck in her brain as soon as she had looked it up, and she had rung it many times. On the third ring Alice answered. Pauline hung up.

'Just having a chat with my mate,' she

said as the dietician and his girlfriend came through the door in white tennis clothes with grass stains and a faint smell of sweat. They didn't look at her as they took the stairs two at a time, laughing at something. Pauline went slowly after them and finished off the last of the ham sandwiches from supper in Daffodil.

'She's gone, that little lady.' Pauline jerked a thumb towards the place where Mrs Rosenbaum had sat. It was the following afternoon. Alice made her heart blank, and looked down at her book.

'Having a nice read?'

Pauline tipped the book forward. 'Janette Turner Hospital. She must be the same as me.'

'She's Australian, I think.' Alice didn't want to be too much of a know-all.

'No, I mean, she must've been found in a hospital, like me. I was left in the toilets at Barts, that's why they give me the name. Pauline after the nurse who found me, and Batholomew after Barts. 'Ere, nice milky one, two sugars.'

'Thanks, Pauline, you're a pal.'

As she drank her tea, Alice realised that she had been given the central fact about

Pauline. That beginning had determined her progression to this institutional job, that overall, the trolley, the table for one in Spud-U-Like, the holidays spent in shopping precincts.

'I had my picture in all the papers,' said Pauline, and Alice saw a crimson, new-born baby waving feeble arms from swaddling clothes of newsprint, on a stone floor under a porcelain pedestal.

'Your mother—did they—did she—?'

Pauline's eyes filled as she shook her head, strands of hair whipping her clamped mouth. 'I've never told anybody that before. Nobody here, I mean. Not that they'd be interested anyway, toffee-nosed lot.'

Alice had noticed that the staff hardly gave Pauline a glance or a word. Poor despised capybara, whose cage everybody walked past.

That revelation led to Alice's following Pauline up the concrete stairs after visiting time, with a sense of danger, knowing she had taken an irrevocable step. She hadn't known how to refuse the long-threatened invitation after Pauline's tears. To her horror Pauline at once took an unopened bottle of Tia Maria from a cupboard in the tiny kitchen, which was a scaled-down replica of the kitchenette at Daffodil.

'Ah, the curtain with the knot in it! At last!' Alice cried, a bit too gaily, as they carried their glasses through. 'Tell me, Pauline, why does it have a knot in it?'

'I'm a fresh-air fiend. All the cooking smells from foreign cooking get trapped in here so I leave my window open and I have to tie the curtain back or it knocks my ornaments off in the wind.'

'I'd imagined a much more sinister—I mean exotic explanation, but I see your balloon-seller's head has been glued back on at some stage.'

Pauline topped them up.

'Mind if I smoke?'

'That's all right, I'll get the ash tray.'

It had been washed but Alice detected a smear of grey under its rim which indicated that Pauline had at least one other visitor, who smoked.

'It's a lovely flat, Pauline. A little palace. You've made it really homely.'

'It is home.'

'Well yes, of course.'

'You haven't seen the bedroom yet, have you?'

Alice gasped. Fifty pairs of eyes stared

at her from the bed; the big eyes of pink and yellow and white and turquoise fluffy toys, and squinting eyes of trolls with long fluorescent hair.

'Meet the Cuddlies,' said Pauline. 'Sometimes I think they're more trouble than all my patients put together."

Alice felt sudden fear, of all the goggle-eyes, the garish nylon fibres, strong enough to strangle. Pauline had lured her here to kill her. Get her drunk on Tia Maria and do away with her. In cahoots with Kevin.

'What a wonderful collection. Well, I suppose I'll have to think about going, Pauline. Long journey and all that.' Oh God. That was the mistake people always made in films; saying they were going instead of just making a run for it when the murderer was off-guard.

'Oh, I was going to do us a pizza. Won't take a minute in the microwave.' Pauline was bitterly disappointed. That was what friends did, ate pizza on the sofa in front of the telly. Then her face broke into a smile when Alice said, 'OK, great. Thanks, that would be lovely. Mind if I use your loo?'

'Help yourself.'

As Alice left the room she paused, 'Pauline, mind if I ask you something?

Kevin, are you and he...I mean does he come here sometimes?'

'Not often.' Pauline was upset at the intrusion of Kevin into the evening. 'I let him come up once in a while. Only when I'm really browned-off.'

Cheesed-off. Browned-off. Alice had an image of Pauline's brown and yellow overall bubbling in a microwaved Welsh Rarebit.

Pauline put Kevin out of her mind and went into the kitchen as Alice closed the bathroom door behind her. She selected two pizzas from the tiny freezer and got a sharp knife from the drawer to score along the marked quarters. The doorbell rang.

Alice, in the bathroom with her ear to the wall, heard the freezer door slam, and the metallic scrape of cutlery. The doorbell. In total panic she wrenched open the bathroom door. Kevin stood inside the front door, blocking the way. And Pauline had a long knife in her hand.

Alice made a rush for the door, shoving Kevin out of the way but Pauline was right behind her, grabbing the back of her sweatshirt, saying, 'Alice, wait! What about the pizzas?' Alice was pulled round, and for black moments all three were struggling together in the narrow hallway in a tangle of bodies and knife. Then the knife got shoved in. Five inches of stainless steel straight to the heart.

They looked at her lying there. There was no question that she was dead.

'Bloody hell,' said Kevin. 'I only come up for a cup of sugar.'

It occurred to neither of them to call the police.

'I'll have to get her bagged-up,' said Kevin then.

The Domestic was red-eyed and shaky in the morning as she handed out the breakfasts. She looked as if she'd been up all night. She had; the accusing whispers of the Cuddlies had not let up. She could hear them still through her open window as she crossed the grass, the window with the curtain with the knot in it. Her hair was lank and uncombed under her scrunched rufflette of gingham, but nobody gave her a glance anyway.

'Come on Dolly Daydream, let's be having you,' she said with her abrupt mirthless laugh. 'Tea up. Nice milky one, two sugars.'

Once not so long ago, Alice's father, the former Detective Inspector, who was

255

trained to observe, would have looked up with a pleased, though puzzled smile, noticing something amiss as she handed him his tea. She had always had a soft spot for him too, but now he didn't know her from a bar of soap.

Gambling on Ganymede

James Melville

'Since you ask,' George Moreton said to his visitor, gazing in fascination at her enormous earrings, 'it was a young woman who first interested me in murder. In a direct, personal way, I mean. Obviously, the subject in general has always been apt to grip people's imaginations. The Bible is full of murders, and of insights into the motives of those who break what I suppose we must still consider the ultimate taboo. Jealousy, especially of the sexual variety, greed and vanity loomed as large in biblical times as they do now. Murder is perennially fascinating. That is why the less reputable newspapers pay good money for juicy details, and bookshops have special sections devoted to crime fiction and accounts of notorious killers.'

'Right,' the journalist said, and then after a tiny hesitation muttered, 'Excuse me,' in apparent embarrassment, fumbling in her bag and taking out a small powder compact. Opening it, she briefly examined her reflection, noticed nothing untoward about it and closed the compact again. Her interviewee was still staring at her and she fidgeted uneasily. 'Um, is something wrong?'

Moreton shook his head briefly and his eyes met hers at last. 'So impolite,' he said with a smile that transformed his saturnine features. 'I do apologise, Miss Huxtable. I was intrigued by the size of your earrings. I keep expecting them to tear loose from their moorings. Very striking, but aren't they painful to wear?'

'Of course not. They're fashionable.' Sue Huxtable had gone to a good deal of trouble to persuade Nether Burdock's resident celebrity to agree to talk to her, so she made an effort and smiled back. George Everard Moreton was a wrinkly: in his mid-fifties according to his entry in *Who's Who*. So it would be surprising if he *was* switched on. The thought reminded her to switch on the tape recorder she had brought with her and been given permission to use. After checking the sound levels she leaned forward with a bright, professional smile.

'Let's go back a bit, Mr Moreton.

I'd like to ask you about your family background. You were born in Malaya, I believe.'

'I was, yes. My father was in the Colonial Service.'

'And your mother?'

'Her name was Amy. She was the only child of a judge. I can remember my grandfather. A nice old man who smelt of tobacco. He sometimes took his false teeth out after meals. As a little boy I thought this a wizard trick and I tried hard to do it myself. Couldn't understand why my own refused to budge.'

'Sir George Everard. You were named after him.'

'Least my parents could do. I learned years later that he set up what was at the time a generous trust fund to provide for my education and that of my younger brother Richard. I expect you disapprove?'

Sue Huxtable did, but was fair-minded enough to accept that the old chap could hardly be blamed personally for having been born with a silver spoon sticking out of his mouth. She shrugged and shook her head.

'How old were you when you came to England?'

259

'Two. My father was reassigned to the Colonial Office in London in 1937 and we lived there until the outbreak of war. My grandfather died soon after. Left my mother his house in Northamptonshire, and she took us two young boys to live there while Father remained in London.' Moreton paused and rubbed his long nose thoughtfully. 'Odd, really. There was a Northamptonshire aspect to this murder case I began telling you about.'

'There was a girl involved, you said.'

'Mm.' A faraway look came into his eyes. 'Priscilla Danvers. A stunner. She had lovely deep blue eyes and a gorgeous figure. I was awfully keen on her. Met her soon after I went up to Cambridge.'

'Chichele College, wasn't it?' Moreton detected the note of condescension in her voice, and gave her a sharp look. Sue gazed back at him equably, satisfied by his reaction and reflecting that it would teach him to make remarks about earrings.

After a pregnant pause, Moreton returned her question with another. 'May I ask where *you* were educated, Miss Huxtable?'

'I took my degree at Essex. In sociology and environmental studies.'

Moreton said something under his breath. Sue thought it might have been 'Good God' and prepared to bristle, but was disarmed as he went on in an audible voice. 'You're right about Chichers, I fear. My brother Richard's the brainy one. My own academic career was singularly undistinguished. I barely scraped through Common Entrance, and exasperated my teachers at Tonbridge.'

'Why?'

'They suggested acidly in their reports that the principal explanation for my generally lacklustre performance even in the subjects I enjoyed was simple indolence.'

'And was it?'

'Oh, I expect so. I was a scrawny, weedy youth, equally lethargic on the sports field, so there wasn't much to be done with me. I usually kept afloat, just, and considered myself lucky to get to Cambridge at all. The dons at Chichele weren't all duds, you know. I read philosophy and history, and met a man called Hitchcock who inspired in me a lifelong interest in an admiration for the philosopher Thomas Hobbes. I'm working on a monograph about him,' he added shyly. 'I don't suppose it will ever be published.'

Sue knew little about Hobbes beyond the fact that he had described something or somebody as 'nasty, brutish and short' but nodded in understanding and murmured encouragingly. It was comfortable in Moreton's study, the coffee was excellent and her host showed no sign of impatience, but it was time to turn to his achievements as an amateur detective.

'So you met Priscilla Danvers. Not at Chichele College, surely?'

'On the stairs there, actually. She was a post-graduate student at Newnham, but acted as a research assistant to one of the dons at my college. Rupert Young his name was. University lecturer in the history of art. He had rooms on the same staircase as mine.' Moreton sighed and crossed his long legs. 'It was love at first sight on my part; but in those decorous days I was too shy to tell her so.'

'Is she why several of the cases you've solved have an art history background? Like the Case of the Old Pretender recently?'

Moreton smiled, privately gratified that the case in question had been so named by the tabloid press. 'I haven't thought about it. Perhaps. Look, do you want to hear about my first brush with murder, or not?'

'Please.' Sue found herself warming to George Everard Moreton, CBE, who had on her arrival at his house a few miles from Cambridge struck her as being stuffy and pompous, every inch the retired diplomat. Whether or not he had been scrawny and weedy in his youth he was now spare and elegant, and his air of settled melancholy was rather appealing.

'More coffee? No? So be it.' He poured a second cup for himself and settled back in his chair. 'Well, Priscilla accepted one or two of my timid invitations, out of politeness I suppose, but she displayed no particular interest in me. Until Rupert Young was murdered, that is, and my neighbour on the same landing was charged with the crime.'

'Do you mind if I smoke?' Sue blurted out, and instantly regretted it when she saw the expression on her host's face.

'Not at all,' he murmured, rising at once from his chair and fetching a small cut-glass bowl from a cupboard under the bookshelves that lined one wall of the room. 'You may use this as an ashtray.' Sue took out her cigarettes and lighter but willed herself to abstain. Observing her forbearance, Moreton raised one bushy eyebrow, but made no comment and after a short pause went on with his story.

'My neighbour was an American; a beautiful young man called Howard Stoner. He was a Bostonian, with exquisite manners. He always made me feel noisy, vulgar and demonstrative. Anyway, Howard went to Dr Young's rooms by appointment for a tutorial and discovered him slumped over his desk with a dagger sticking out of his back. I gather it was a souvenir of Young's wartime service in a Royal Marine commando unit. Priscilla told me he used it as a paper knife. Howard felt for a pulse and, finding none, went to the porter's lodge and raised the alarm.'

'And Stoner was charged with the murder?'

'Mmm. His Boston brahmin conditioning let him down. The head porter told the police that he strolled up to the lodge "as cool as cucumber" rather than at a run, and reported his discovery in a quiet, conversational way. Everybody in college knew that this was typical of Howard, but the head porter didn't like Americans. His daughter had been "wronged", as he put it, by a GI during the war. Not so very many years before, you must realise.'

'And the police arrested him on the strength of *that?*'

'No, no. There was documentary evidence. Compromising photographs of Stoner and Rupert Young were found in Young's room. Not in the least pornographic. Indeed quite innocent to modern eyes—the two of them outside country pubs in hiking gear smiling at each other happily, that sort of thing—but they established the background, as it were, and made the key item all the more damning. This was a single sheet of paper seemingly pushed hurriedly underneath the blotter on Young's desk. It bore a rough sketch of a Tiepolo drawing depicting Jupiter and Ganymede, and above it an unfinished, scribbled note in Young's handwriting. The note read: *Dearest Howard, this cannot go on*— I need hardly tell *you* the implications, but the police failed to grasp them at first, until an officer with a classical education enlightened them.'

The blank expression in Sue's face gradually faded as Moreton went on. 'The myth, you will remember, has Jupiter taking a fancy to Ganymede and carrying him off to, er, enjoy him. In former centuries wealthy men with homosexual proclivities frequently commissioned artists to produce works which reminded informed viewers of the story.'

'Wow,' Sue said thoughtfully.

'Wow indeed. I'll just remind you that this was about the time of the Wolfenden Report recommending the decriminalisation of homosexual acts between consenting male adults, but before the law was altered in consequence. Rupert Young was widely known to be, in the quaint usage of the time, "musical" or "a confirmed bachelor", but possibly because of his war record—he'd done something mysterious but brave in the Balkans, won a DSO and was thought of as a latter-day Lawrence of Arabia—he was far from being the butt of tasteless humour. Once the light had dawned on them, the police arrived at the not unreasonable conclusion that Young had decided to end his relationship with Stoner, who killed him out of desperation. Howard Stoner steadfastly protested his innocence, but admitted under questioning that Young had advanced substantial sums of money to him. That is to say, he had exploited the older man's infatuation by leading him on in the expectation of favours to come. This explanation availed him little: scrutiny of Young's bank statements revealed just how much money had changed hands, raising the possibility of blackmail at the very least. The cumulative evidence was so damning that Stoner was charged with murder and remanded in custody for trial at the Assizes.' Moreton smiled again. 'Another relic of bygone days, I'm afraid.'

'But you're going to tell me he wasn't guilty.'

'I must admit that most of us thought he was. From the first, however, Priscilla was certain that Howard was innocent, and she enlisted my help to prove it. Do you know what a scout is?'

Sue looked puzzled. 'You mean a Boy Scout?'

'Not in the context of a Cambridge college. No, a scout is or was the servant who cleans rooms, makes beds, and, provided he—they were invariably men in the old days—is treated with sufficient generosity, acts to some extent as a personal valet. Hot water for shaving, morning tea, that sort of thing. Howard Stoner and I, with Rupert Young and others, shared the services of a Mr Ernie Biggleswade. Ernie was a spry little man who, like most of his kind, probably knew more about his gentlemen than they did themselves. He would never have discussed Dr Young's affairs with a young woman, needless to say, but at Priscilla's request I sought his support for a hypothesis that she advanced to me.'

Sue Huxtable wished Moreton would come to the point more directly, but found herself savouring his leisurely way of telling the story. So she remained silent, merely nodding encouragingly.

'I may say that I was less than pleased by Priscilla's approach, which I'm afraid I assumed was motivated by affection for Howard Stoner. He *was* extremely good looking, and people of my generation weren't as apt to query a person's sexuality as they are now. I thought Priscilla might at some stage have persuaded herself that she had a chance with Stoner. However that may be, she explained to me that as Young's research assistant, she was acquainted with some of his associates outside the university, including a certain art dealer called Hughes. Young was a considerable authority in his field, and was called upon from time to time to pronounce on the authenticity or otherwise of drawings whose attribution was dubious. For his opinions he was of course paid well, but Priscilla suspected that for the money Hughes offered he occasionally went further.'

'And authenticated fakes?'

'Precisely.' Moreton gazed down at his hands for a moment, and when he spoke again it was at a brisker pace. 'I'm sorry, I'm dragging this out intolerably. Suffice it to say that Ernie Biggleswade the scout confirmed that Hughes had from time to time visited Rupert Young in his rooms.'

Sue was taken aback when the elegant Mr Moreton then displayed an unexpected talent for mimicry. 'Biggleswade described Hughes as a "shifty bloke, Mr Moreton, wouldn't trust 'im farther than I could throw 'im," and when I asked him if he thought Stoner had indeed murdered Young, he poo-poohed the idea. "Not 'im, sir. Wouldn't 'urt a fly. Easily led and extravagant, yes, and a born racing tipster's mug. Besides, Dr Young was fool enough to settle his debts for 'im. Why would 'e want to kill the goose what laid the golden eggs?" Biggleswade pointed out.'

'I see. But of course Young might have told Stoner he'd decided not to pay his gambling debts any longer. That would have made Stoner mad, and...anyway, Priscilla Danvers thought this dealer, Hughes, had something to do with it?'

'She did, and after I'd been half-persuaded of Stoner's innocence by Ernie Biggleswade, I agreed to accompany her to Bedlington Hall, a stately home in Northamptonshire, to test her theory. Priscilla had a car, something almost unheard of for a single young woman in those days, and which contributed significantly to her glamour, I suppose. What clinched the matter for me was that my mother was still living in what had become the family home less than fifteen miles away, and I planned to introduce Priscilla to her. She'd told me that her father was a VIP in the City, master of one of the livery companies, and I was sure my mother would thoroughly approve of her.'

'Beautiful *and* rich! And what did she expect to find at Bedlington Hall?'

Moreton looked at Sue Huxtable with a gratified smile. 'I say, you do have a gift for encouraging me to run on. Like those chaps in Plato's dialogues who keep saying things like "Yes, indeed," or "How can that be?" to keep Socrates on the go. Do you find this boring?'

It was Sue's turn to smile. 'No, *indeed,*' she said in what she hoped was the manner of one of Socrates's entourage, inviting him with a little gesture to continue.

'Well, Priscilla told me that in recent weeks Rupert Young had paid several visits to Bedlington Hall in the company of Hughes. He told her about the first one, without mentioning Hughes, explaining that he'd been to see a collection of drawings they had in their archives. It had been assembled by an eighteenth-century aristocrat who had owned the place. Young reported that in his view there was little of interest in the collection, but Priscilla sensed that he was more excited than he pretended to be, and noticed on his desk a sketch he'd made of Jupiter and Ganymede in the style of Tiepolo: the one subsequently found by the police and shown to Stoner when they questioned him. So when a few days later Young slunk off again rather furtively and kept her in the dark about his movements she decided to follow him on the next occasion. And lo, Dr Young went to Bedlington Hall in a car driven by Hughes, discreetly pursued by Priscilla.'

'It was clever of her to avoid being spotted.'

'Not really. Bedlington Hall is open to the public most days, and even at that time it boasted a car park for the use of visitors. When Priscilla and I went there were several other vehicles in it. Hughes might even have been keeping a watch on us for all I know. If he was, he would have seen Priscilla kiss me enthusiastically and at length before we left the car and went inside. I was thrilled, needless to say.'

'Well, come on. What did you do at Bedlington Hall?'

'We paid our money and Priscilla asked the lady at the ticket desk if we might have a word with Major Hoskins. Priscilla had done her homework and discovered that he was the part-time librarian at Bedlington Hall. Knowing his name did the trick: I think the ticket lady, a formidable old trout, nourished a *tendresse* for the Major. At all events, she disappeared and came back in a minute or two with him in tow, blushing and simpering girlishly.'

'Major Hoskins was? That must have impressed you.'

'Now, now, Miss Huxtable. I don't know the details of the Major's military career, but he struck me as a charmingly vague old buffer when we met him. Susceptible, too, and who can blame him. Priscilla was wearing a pale blue, tightly fitting, fluffy mohair button-through sweater with a flared white skirt, I remember. She had an alice band in her hair, her eyes were sparkling and she looked marvellous. Hoskins clearly took a fancy to her, nodding and smiling benignly while she explained her academic credentials and asked if we might be shown the collection of drawings. He agreed at once and pottered off with her. I brought up the rear, not before noting that the ticket lady's expression was distinctly woebegone.' Moreton shifted in his chair and glanced at his watch.

'Heavens, I *have* run on, haven't I? I'm sorry. Anyway, there isn't much more to tell. The Major was as putty in Priscilla's hands, and indiscreet to boot. Took us to the library, which he rather unnecessarily explained was not one of the rooms open to the public. It had once been grand, but had gone to seed. Holes in the curtains, stuffing coming out of Louis Quinze furniture, the carpet badly worn and even a bucket in one corner catching drips from a leaky ceiling. I chiefly remember the pervasive smell of damp old parchment and Hoskins blundering about, knocking over a framed photograph on his work-table.' Moreton paused and re-crossed his legs, carefully hitching up his trouser leg to preserve the crease.

'Well, to cut a long story short, he showed us the drawings. The one in question was a pretty little thing, I thought, but I'm no connoisseur now and was totally ignorant then. Hoskins explained with enthusiasm that it had recently been examined several times by an eminent scholar at the request of a London dealer who had tentatively identified it as being the work of Tiepolo; and he and the owner were encouraged to hope that an attractive offer might be forthcoming. He seemed not to have heard that Rupert Young had been killed. Priscilla and I took our leave in high good humour, agreeing that there was a pretty strong chance that Hughes had been blackmailing Young into providing a false authentication, with a view to making a small fortune for himself. At Priscilla's instigation, and of course with my supporting testimony, the police interviewed Hughes who admitted nothing at first. However, the subsequent official investigation into his affairs produced evidence of the complicity with Young —whose indiscretions in pre-war Germany left him vulnerable, to say the least—in all manner of international frauds on American museums and private collectors. When Hughes committed suicide it was as good as an admission of guilt. So Howard Stoner was exonerated and the file was closed.'

Moreton gave a little sigh and opened his hands to suggest to Sue Huxtable that his story was at an end. She took the hint, switched off her tape recorder and began to gather her things together. Then she paused, struck by something about her host's expression. 'May I ask what happened to Priscilla Danvers? Did you introduce her to your mother?'

He nodded. 'Indeed I did. Mother behaved impeccably as always, made her welcome and said all the right things. But I could tell that she didn't take to Priscilla, which surprised me. It made no difference in the end, because within a month Priscilla told me that she and Howard Stoner were to be married and would make their home in Boston.'

'Oh dear. You must have been upset.'

'I was, of course, and at first I behaved rather foolishly, attempting to make her change her mind by reminding her about Howard's supposed proclivities. She, um, well, not to put too fine a point on it, she indicated that I was talking bosh and that Stoner had many times demonstrated to her personal satisfaction that he was perfectly normal. That set me wondering why Priscilla had been generally so agreeable to me lately, and positively passionate in the car, and I formulated and set out to test an alternative hypothesis to account for everything that had happened.'

Moreton's calm, unflappable manner seemed momentarily to have deserted him, and he twisted his hands together in apparent mental discomfort.

'I checked *Who's Who*. As I'd expected, her father was in it, and it gave her mother's maiden name, Hoskins. A simple coincidence perhaps, but on the other hand maybe the librarian at Bedlington Hall wasn't so vague as he pretended to be. The more I thought about it the more inconceivable it seemed that he hadn't heard about the murder of Rupert Young, which had been reported in all the papers. Then there was the photograph he'd knocked over. I'd only caught a glimpse of it when I was still elated from Priscilla's embraces, but when I thought about it I remembered that it was of a little blonde girl. On an impulse I telephoned Major Hoskins without giving my name, and with fingers crossed told him I had an urgent message from his...niece. "From Priscilla?" he said, and then I knew for sure that I'd been had by the pair of them. I put the phone down, leaving him I hope in a genuine state of agitation, and confronted Priscilla.'

Sue Huxtable stood as if transfixed, her mouth slightly open as Moreton went on.

'I told her I knew that she and her uncle had conspired to set up the whole thing, and that Stoner had been their willing accomplice in a scheme to sell off the "Tiepolo", complete with letters of authentication provided by Young, to a wealthy American museum. Priscilla listened without a flicker of emotion as I went on to say that I suspected her of being the one who had first blackmailed and then killed Young when he grew sick of the whole shady enterprise and threatened to expose them. She had the opportunity: she was in and out of Young's rooms every day, *and* she knew the extent to which his other dealings in the art market, not to mention his homosexuality, laid him open to pressure. I accused her of being well aware that Hughes's discreditable activities wouldn't stand up to scrutiny and of setting out to frame him, using me as an innocent tool. At the end of my recital Priscilla just smiled and said "Lucky for us he committed suicide, wasn't it, then?" I never saw her again.'

'That's *terrible.*'

'Mm. Still, look at it this way, I'm not sure I would have liked being married to a murderess. Not that Priscilla would have had me, in any case.'

'But...didn't you go to the police?'

'What would have been the point? Young was dead, Hughes was dead, and I was the only witness to the conversation with her uncle. It would have been my word against theirs. I cheered myself up by telling myself that Priscilla and Stoner probably deserved each other. And as Hobbes pointed out, revenge is merely "a retribution of Evil for Evil". Wouldn't you agree?'

Notes on the Contributors

Gwendoline Butler is the creator of Inspector Coffin and was the recipient of the Crime Writers' Association Silver Dagger Award with *A Coffin for Pandora*. She also writes as Jennie Melville, a pseudonym she uses for her gothic mysteries and for the exploits of the Windsor based policewoman, Charmian Daniels. A graduate of Lady Margaret Hall, she has been a writer for many years with over forty novels to her credit.

Desmond Cory is the pseudonym of Shaun McCarthy, a highly talented and versatile thriller writer, perhaps best known for his psychological satire, *The Circe Complex*. He has spent much of his life as a Professor of English and is currently teaching in Eastern Turkey. When not involved with the academic life he spends his time in Spain or Wales and is currently working on a new Professor Dobie mystery.

Clare Curzon has worked as an interpreter, translator, teacher, probation officer and social secretary, but she is above all a writer. As Rhona Petrie she is author of traditionally serpentine whodunnits, as Marie Buchanan she is an historical novelist and as herself she has created the highly acclaimed series of mysteries featuring the team of Thames Valley policemen led by Superintendent Mike Yeadings.

Antonia Fraser is well known for such historical biographies as *Mary, Queen of Scots* and for her series of mysteries featuring the television reporter Jemima Shore. The creation of Jemima stemmed from her creator's early addiction to crime fiction and from admiration of such women writers as Dorothy L Sayers, Ruth Rendell and Patricia Highsmith. Married to the playwright Harold Pinter, she lives in London.

Tim Heald is a journalist, biographer and cricket chronicler as well as a mystery writer. In the latter field he is the creator of Board of Trade investigator, Simon Bognor, who always gets his man but is not entirely faithful to his wife, who is plain but long suffering of her husband's habits of smoking, drinking and taking no exercise. Tim Heald considers his novels are pretty funny and is easily upset when critics don't see the jokes.

Reginald Hill was a teacher until turning to full-time writing in 1981. His series of crime novels featuring the Yorkshire policemen Dalziel and Pascoe have attracted much critical acclaim, a large following and the Crime Writers' Association Gold Dagger Award. He is a master-craftsman of the short story and has also had his plays broadcast on radio and television.

Graham Ison spent most of his working life as a policeman, not only as beat copper and detective, but also in the Diplomatic Protection Squad and Special Branch. He was personal detective to both Edward Heath and Harold Wilson, and has used his experiences to dramatic effect in his crime novels. After a lifetime of policing in London he and his wife have now settled in Hampshire.

Peter Lovesey's first novel, *Wobble to*

Death, won a competition for the best first mystery. It was also the debut of Sergeant Cribb and Constable Thackeray, a duo who successfully translated to the small screen. *The False Inspector Dew* won the Gold Dagger Award and *Waxwork* the Silver. Recently he has turned his remarkable talents to the contemporary detective novel with his creation of Peter Diamond, a thoroughly irascible ex-policeman of the old school who does not believe that genetic fingerprinting and computers are as infallible as his colleagues do, preferring instead to use the art of deduction to stunning effect.

Shena Mackay has written seven novels and two collections of short stories. Her first two published novellas were written when she was in her teens. Many of her stories have been broadcast, and she has written for radio. Her latest novel *Dunedin* appeared this year, and she is a book reviewer and journalist.

James Melville's career as a cultural diplomat created the mature and felicitous offshoot of Superintendent Otani of the Japanese police. In a series of mysteries which are highly respected as first class whodunnits, James Melville also portrays the mores of Japanese society with authority and affection, thereby informing as well as entertaining his many readers. He retired from diplomatic life in 1983 and now lives in Norfolk.

This Large Print Book for the Partially sighted, who cannot read normal print, is published under the auspices of

THE ULVERSCROFT FOUNDATION

THE ULVERSCROFT FOUNDATION

. . . we hope that you have enjoyed this Large Print Book. Please think for a moment about those people who have worse eyesight problems than you . . . and are unable to even read or enjoy Large Print, without great difficulty.

You can help them by sending a donation, large or small to:

**The Ulverscroft Foundation,
1, The Green, Bradgate Road,
Anstey, Leicestershire, LE7 7FU,
England.**

or request a copy of our brochure for more details.

The Foundation will use all your help to assist those people who are handicapped by various sight problems and need special attention.

Thank you very much for your help.